LET ME PIMP
OR
LET ME DIE

Till Game Do Us Part

Caujuan Akim Mayo

This is a work of fiction. Names, characters, places and incidents are either the product of the authors imagination or are used fictitiously. Any resemblance to actual events or locales or persons, living or dead is entirely coincidental.

From The Mind Of

Caujuan Akim Mayo
aka
Ka$hanova

ISBN-13: 978-0615724256
ISBN-10: 0615724256

LCCN:

ACKNOWLEDGMENTS

=Family=

First off I would like to thank my mother Queen. Without you, none of this would be possible. You've stuck by me through thick and thin and never turned your back on me from day one. You should be an inspiration for other mothers and mothers to be. You are the true meaning of unconditional love. Smile and be proud, "My Original Black Queen" you've done well. To my son Raa'Quan, you're the very reason why I stay strong and focused, slowed down in the streets, and got my act together. It's been me and you since day one. A father and son could get no closer. The bond that we have will last forever. To my adopted son Duff.E aka "mini me" I'm proud of the man you've become. To my brother Allmighty, look how we still made it. In early 2000 we changed the game, now look at all these dudes tryna catch up. 13 years...Yeah right, try 2 and a wake up. Ha ha ha ha, eat that haters. To Reality, you had me nervous for a minute bro, but I'm glad you slowed down while still keeping it "G," My brother Self, you grew up and followed your own path, I'm proud of you for that. Thanks for helping take care of my son and picking up where I left off when I went to jail. To my brother Hakiem, congratulations on the new edition. I see it helped you grow up further. To my brother Rayshon, hey bro, you're always gonna be "lil Bits" to me, ha ha ha. To my cousin Kemo, you're still my #1 relative. We've been doing our thing since we was knee high to a grass hopper. To my sister Yanai, I'm proud of you for not letting the streets take you under. When all of your friends was having sex and giving it away, you was a virgin and saving it for the same man you're with today. To my sister Asia, even though I don't get to say it enough, I miss and love you always. To all my nieces and nephews, so many to name so I'll just say that I equally love you all the same. To aunt Jeannie, you have a heart of gold and I appreciate you as well. To my aunt Laqueesha, words can't begin to express the love that I have for you. You've always been like a second mother to me. I know there is "nothing" that I can ask of you that's within your reach that you wouldn't do for me. And last but not least, To my grandma Roselyn Lane, may you forever Rest in Peace! One Love

=Friends=

My two realist hommiez, Redlite and Phero. There's no way I could have made it on the run without ya'll. I look at you two as brothers not friends. When this book do numbers, I got you Phero. Death before dishonor. Bogard, Jay Jay, Kadeve, you proved to be a real hommie as well and I'll never forget what you did for me. Good luck on the music (not that you need it). To the Skyline hommiez, wayyy too many to name you all so let me just give up a fat "P" and leave it at that. Special Piru Love shout out to YP, Baby Jed, Tank.Bo, Slikk Rick, Big June, Bullet, D.Roll and Big Red (Gunn). I love ya'll hommie! To all the brothers and sisters locked down behind them walls, keep your head up. To all the real Pimps, Players, Macks and Hoes in the game, I'm not gonna dry snitch like some, name drop and call you out. So we'll just leave it like this...Chuuuch! Special shout out to the Daygo Macks representing in a real way. Gotta give it up to Too Real For TV, Michael Maroy. You're a real nigga, thanks for everything. Gotta give a shout out to the game that made me. Don't forget that, the two realist niggas outta Daygo to ever do it first was Ka$hanova Tha Mack & $upreme. When niggas was still on them concrete streets, we was in them executive suites, Holla!

=Haters=

Gotta give a super shout out to all the haters. You're the reason all this was possible. Ya'll was the motivation behind my pen. I'd like to thank the mutha fucka's that locked me up, which gave me time to write. The sheriffs, detectives, and all law enforcement that went out their way for "years" to take down my family. Now you can finally retire, but not before I get this check, ha ha ha, I'm laughing straight to the bank with this! To the bitches that fell off during my incarceration, picture me rollin! To all the hatin ass niggas and bitches, and one big FUCK YOU! to you dirty rat snitches.

Now that I have your attention...Let's read.

1 GRADUATION DAY

Ricky Walters grew up during the roaring 80's, the height of the gang bang era. His brother was a blood who was killed in a bloody drive-by when he was 16 years old at a blood picnic. His father, an ex pimp that walked out on the family in the late 70's when Ricky was just 4 years old.

His mother was a hard working single parent of two, excluding his dead brother. In 1980, Ricky's mother moved from Chicago to San Diego California searching for a better life. Ricky was just six years old when they moved to San Diego, so to him, this was the only life he'd ever known, or at least remembers...

1994

(Clapping and cheers!!!) "Yeah, congratulations!"

"Thanks mom."

"I'm so proud of you. My son, graduated from high school."

Ricky beat the odds. Attending the Blood infested Morse high school for 4 years and graduating without following in his late brothers tracks as a gang member. After his brothers death, Ricky vowed that he would never get involved with gangs.

"You look so handsome in your cap and gown," his mother expressed proudly.

"He look al'ight," his sister said sarcastically.

"Shut up sis." They both laughed.

As a graduation gift, Ricky's mother bought her son a 510 wagon on McLeans. It took her 2 years to save up for it but she promised herself as well as Ricky that if he graduated high school on time, she would buy him a car, and that was the car of his dreams.

"Well son, I have a surprise for you." she handed him the keys and pointed to the 510 sitting in the parking lot.

"Yeah! that's what I'm talkin bout," Ricky said with excitement as he hugged and kissed his mother on the cheek. Ricky jumped in his new car and fired up the engine. This was his first car, so to him, it was like starting up a brand new cadillac and he loved it more than life itself.

2 GAME TIME

The long hot days began to take a toll on Ricky as he contemplated quitting his security job. It's been 6 months since he graduated and the thought of standing in one place guarding an empty warehouse for 8 hours in the hot sun had finally taken it's toll.

"Damn it's hotter than a mutha fucka!" Ricky said to himself while wiping off a small bead of sweat on his forehead. At that moment, Ricky knew today would be his last day as a rent-a-cop. After his shift was over, he handed in his flashlight and quit.

Ricky drove down the 5 freeway and got off on Palomar in Chula Vista. He was on his way down to One Stop Auto on Broadway. A one stop shop for getting your car hooked up. He was going to get his windows tinted and system put in.

An ex pimp name Trust owned the shop. Trust was a pimp turned business man. He really had his shit together. Back in the day Trust was one of the baddest pimps out of San Diego. What made him get rich so quick was the fact that he had nothing but white bitches. The finest that money could afford. Not only that, but he was street smart as well as business savvy. He treated the game as a means to an end and wouldn't stop until he had enough money to retire and go legit.

Ricky didn't know it at the time, but meeting Trust would change his life forever.

Ricky pulled into One Stop Auto and honked the horn for the owner or sales rep.

"Hello may I help you?"

"Yeah, I'm looking to get my windows tinted and system put in."

"Okay, well you came to the right place. Why don't you come inside and pick out an amp, speakers and deck. We can start from there, unless you already have a system and just need me to install it."

"Naw I don't have anything. I need the works. I've been saving up for 6 months just to get the baddest system that money can buy."

"Alright, well how many watts you looking to push?"

"At least a 1000, maybe 2."

"Shit, in that 510, that's gonna bump! Bitches a be sure to hear you coming at least a block away." normally Trust would talk to his customers more professional, but with Ricky, game recognized game and he saw something in youngster that was different from the rest. Kinda like when a thug sees a plain clothes cop in the streets, even without his uniform on you can still tell he's a cop just by the way he carries himself. Ricky went in the shop and picked out what he wanted. "I'll take those 10 inch

Kickers, that 1,200 watt Kicker amp, with that Sony faceless."

"Good choice. That's about $1,700. I'll hook you up with that, plus installation for $1,200."

"And the tint?"

"How dark you want it?"

"Limo, I wouldn't want you to be able to see me in the daylight with a flashlight."

Hahaha, I like this little nigga, Trust thought to himself. "Alright, I'll do everything for $1,500."

"That's wuss up." Ricky was prepared to pay $2,000 so he felt good knowing he just saved $500 bucks. As Trust began to prep Ricks car, Ricky began to think about what he was gonna do now about work, Since he quit his job and spent $1,500 of the money he saved on his car.

He had about $900 left. That's including the $500 He just saved on his system and tint. As Trust hooked up Ricks car, they chopped it up about life in the streets of SD (San Diego). After about 45 minutes into the conversation, Ricky opened up about his brother, then his mother, and then not too long after that his father.

Now one thing about pimps is, they love talking about pimpin. Even ex-pimps no longer in the game. That's when Trust told Ricky about his former self. "Yeah I use ta pimp. I was the coldest pimp that ever lived!" It's funny how all pimps thought that, but Trust actually was. "I had over 10 of the finest white bitches you ever saw. All pulling in at least $500 a day. And this was in the 70's." Rick thought to himself, *By todays standards, that's like a $1000 a day.* "Damn that's some long bread." The only people Rick knew who made money like that was D-Boys. Straight dope dealers. He kept listening. By this point, Trust was in Rick's good ear, and he was soaking up game like a sponge. "So how you get a female to go out there, sell her body, and then bring you back all the money?"

"Ahhh, the #1 question." Trust responded with a smirk. "First of all young blood, this game gotta be in you not on you." Trust was in full pimp mode now. "You see here young blood, a bitch a do anything for her man when she loves him, but even more importantly, when she trust and respects him. That's already in her nature. That's why believe it or not women are a thousand times more loyal than men."

Each word that Trust spoke illuminated Ricks brain with wisdom, and the more Trust spoke, the more Rick wanted to learn.

"You see young blood, pimps is born not made. You ever had a girlfriend cheat on you and at the end of the day it didn't faze you the least? Or a girl you might have shared with your patnas, ran a train together and the whole nine yards without catching feelings?" Before Ricky could answer, Trust continued. "But here's the kicker," Trust came from inside the 510, looked Ricky dead in his eyes and said, "could you let the woman you actually love with all your heart, fuck your best friend, let him have her any and every way an position imaginable, come home and get in the shower then climb in the bed next to you like nothing happened? If the answer is yes, then you can pimp. If the answer is no, then you're better off falling in love, getting married, and working a square job at Wendy's."

That was deep, Ricky thought to himself, but the game didn't stop there. "Now the key to being a good pimp is to control a bitches mind. If you have the mind then you have the body." Ricky kept listening, taking mental note of every word.

"See a bitch needs guidance by nature. Even square women. That's why when a hoe, as well as a square woman, has a good pimp or man that knows what he's doing in life, focused, wise and always knows the right steps to take and moves to make, there's no holding them back. Bonnie and Clyde all the way." The more Trust talked, the more Ricky felt like what he was saying made sense.

"Now I'm a get deep young blood. You have a lot of haters out there, and haters are a pimps worst enemy. A pimp is the most hated individual on earth. For a number of reasons." As trust laid part of the tint across the back window and smoothed it out, he continued what he was saying. "1st...men hate pimps because the majority of them are tricks. So they hate the fact that they have to pay for something that the pimp gets for free. Not only that, but then after tricking and spending his hard earned cash on the bitch, she turns around and gives it all to a pimp. Now his money's in another mans pocket. Cold shot! Reason why women hate pimps is something totally different. Believe it or not a lot of women are actually intrigued with pimpin and very curious. That's why it's so easy for a seasoned pimp to turn out a square bitch. Truth of the matter is, every bitch has thought about hoe'n at least one time, even ya momma."

What! "my" mother? Ricky questioned to himself. Then he thought about his dad and how he was a pimp. He couldn't help but wonder what type of roll his mother played in "that" relationship when they were together. "Yep, even your momma. This shit goes back to the beginning of time. Shit, it's even in the bible. Women were hoe'n before Christ was born."

Wow that's deep thought Ricky, but Trust was right. Mary Magdalene was a prostitute.

"So you see young blood, as long as there's women walking this earth, there will be prostitutes. What women hate about pimpin is the fact that a hoe is paying a pimp for something she can do herself." Trust continued speaking as he began to measure and lay a piece of tint on one of the side windows. "But it's not about that. She's paying for the guidance as well as the companionship of a like minded individual. What other type a man could a hooker be with other than a pimp, a square? Dude wouldn't except her as she is. It would break his heart to know that every night the love of his life is sleeping with other men for money."

"So what do you mean by guidance?"

"Well young blood, most women don't know how to manage money. As quick as they make it, they're at the mall, hair and nail salon spending it up. A pimp is gonna stack the money knowing that there's gonna be some ups and downs, just like a roller coaster in the game. Then when the bread grow and they have enough money set aside for bail, lawyers and a rainy day, that's when they go splurging. Then when they do spend, they do it big. It takes a lot of discipline young blood."

Sounds easy enough, thought Ricky. It was no different then when he saved most of his money from his security job until he had enough to trick out his ride. Made perfect sense to him. Ricky was stuck on Trust every word. The more trust spoke the more Ricky wanted to know. By this time, Trust was just about done with the tint. All that was left was the install of the amp and speakers which he had saved for last. That way the tint could dry during the install. Trust laid the final piece of tint on the front side window, shut the doors and headed for the trunk.

"So how much does a pimp get when a hoe turns a date...1/2?"

"Hahahaha!" Trust broke out laughing due to Ricks question and said, "not unless she wants 1/2 of this pimpin."

Now Ricky was confused. Why would a hoe go out, sell her body, then give "all" her money away? All the while not having anything to show for the date. Before Ricky could get the question out of his mind and formed into words, Trust explained.

"See like I told you, you have to be the pilot in the situation and she's the co-pilot. Can you fly a plane and properly reach your destination with only 1/2 your fuel? A plane can fly without a co-pilot but never without the pilot. So without you, there's no guidance. And even on auto pilot eventually the plane's gonna run out of gas and crash! This is what she's paying you for. You're like her manager. Not only that, but her lover, father, counselor, financial backer, shit, just say the bitch go to jail, all the money in the world won't bail, "yourself" out. You're gonna need someone to post bond for you. May even need to put up a house or car as collateral. Now if the bitch was renegading," at that point Ricky was confused.

"What's renegading?" asked Ricky.

"A renegade is a hoe that works for herself and doesn't have a pimp. Like I was saying, if the hoe is a renegade and gets caught on the blade by vice and needs to bail out later on that night, then how would she do so without a pimp? Call her square family or friends to do so and reveal she just been picked up for prostitution? Good luck wit dat." *Make sense ta me,* thought Ricky.

"That's the #1 reason why society hates pimps. Because of the fact, that's someone's sister, mother or daughter. But what they fail to realize is, this is by choice not force. Your daughter, "chose" to be with a pimp. I never forced a bitch to do shit she didn't wanna do. That's not pimpin. Now don't get me wrong young blood, you have a ton of gorilla pimps out there which is basically a pimp with no game so he gotta kidnap and force a bitch to be with him, but they never last long. Their days are numbered from the day they stepped foot in the game. It's all about dress and finesse, not black eyes and stress. Pimpin promote prostitution, not boxing. So beat a bitch wit words not violence and you'll last long in this game."

Ricky understood and felt like that made perfect sense. He learned this lesson early on with an ex-girlfriend he had back in the day. Apparently, she had done something to piss him off and he slapped her. Even though they had been together a little over 2 and a 1/2 years, that very slap had ended their relationship.

"See young blood, a man usually only puts his hands on a woman when he's lost for words and runs out of things to say. That's a shot to his ego so he results to putting hands on a bitch. But a real pimp is never lost for words. He always knows the right things to say, even when he's wrong.

Believe it or not, it's actually one of the things that makes him so intriguing." Jackpot nodded his head and said, "I can dig it," totally feeling where Trust was coming from.

"Now this is the #1 thang you wanna avoid like an african punk wit AIDS."

"What's that?"

"If you listen I'll tell you." Ricky just smirked sarcastically like, fuck you!

"Stay away from underage girls, period! I don't care if they're already hoe'n or not. That shit a put you under the penitentiary wit a 100 years. I don't condone that shit either. Leave the children alone. Ain't nothing fly about pedophile pimpin. Step your game up and get a bitch that can make proper choices through a fully developed mind instead of praying on innocent, naive children!"

"Yeah, I agree," said Ricky. Trust continued. "See a lot of pimps don't respect that part of the game. They then in turn give the game a black eye and make us all look bad by fuckin wit minors." At that moment, Ricky thought about his 14 year old sister and knew if he found out a grown man was pimpin on her, he'd wanna kill em. As fascinated as he was with the game, even he knew and felt like there still was limits. And underage girls was definitely at the top of that list.

"Young blood, the best way to prosper and have long jeverty in this game is to always treat your hoe like a queen and you're her king. Because at the end of the day she's still a woman with real woman emotions. A lot of pimps treat their hoes like dogs and that's why every other day they cop-n-blow. But wit me...when I get a bitch, I got a bitch." And with that, Trust finished the final touches on Ricks car. He closed the trunk, got in the driver seat and tested out the new system he had installed. The bass was so deep it was rattling the mirrors, trunk, and knocking ornaments off the shelves in the shop. Trust nodded to the music with a smirk like "yeah, that's that shit." He could definitely see that Ricky was just as pleased by the same head nod and smirk he gave off from the passenger side. With a fist to his mouth with one hand, he gave Trust a pound with the other, and that unspoken but known handshake combo that all brothers give when they greet each other.

By this time it was after 6 p.m. and time for the shop to close. Ricky wanted to know more about the game, so Trust told Ricky, let him close up the shop and he'll tell him all he needed to know. From the rules to how to get a hoe to choose. So Trust closed up the shop and for another 2 and a 1/2 hours laced Rick's shoes with everything he needed to know about pimpin.

3 COP-N-BLOW

The next morning Ricky awoke in his bed with nothing on his mind but pimpin. He was going through everything he had remembered he was told by Trust the previous day. He was eager to get started. As much as he wanted to just jump out there and start pimpin, he knew it wasn't that easy. First he had to find the finest bitch that money couldn't resist. Trust taught him that anything less than a 10 was pointless. He had to play the game to win.

"Where can I find a top notch bitch that I can pull and turn out?" he thought out loud to himself. "Hmmm," and then it hit him! "The mall." He remembered when Trust was talking about how much bitches love to shop, and he also knew that a lot of teenage girls like to go to the mall and hang out. It was a melting pot for bitches. A lot of the girls were young but many was still 18 and over.

With that thought in mind, he got up, got dressed, and headed for Plaza Bonita, the mall located in Paradise Hills.

As Ricky pulled into the parking lot he noticed how full it was. It was saturday afternoon, so he knew it'd be packed. ***Boom...boom!*** Bass blaring bumping Too Short as Ricky rolled slow, creeping through the parking lot leaning to the side, one hand on the steering wheel flossing as he passed the front entrance.

"Alright, time ta park this mutha fucka and do what it do." Ricky parked the 510 wagon and made his way to the front door entrance into the mall. "Ahh yeah it's going down," rubbing his hands like a caveman with a stick trying to produce fire. All Ricky saw was prospects. He had the eye of the tiger and was focused on one thing and one thing only...knocking his first bitch and potential hoe.

Trust told Ricky to focus on white bitches because, "that snow a make your pockets grow." But if a bitch was light bright and almost white, then that was cool too.

Ricky walked towards the escalator and headed upstairs where most of the females liked to hang out, right next to the food court. As the escalator reached the top, he got off and looked around and saw nothing but wall to wall bitches. Most of them looked like they were still in high school so he knew he would have to filter them out.

"Damn, this is gonna be easy pickings here," Ricky said to himself. Ricky walked through the food court and caught the eye of a bad ass asian girl with a couple of her friends. They looked like they were in college or seniors in high school. Either way they looked old enough to fit the bill.

The girls was sitting down eating as Ricky walked by, the asian one smiled and waved. This threw Ricky off because she was so forward which made him break the 3 second rule that a lot of men break, when a woman chooses up out the blue and on the spot, or shows just as much interest in you as you saw in her.

He stood there looking goofy but then snapped out of it quick, smiled, and waved back. Her friends she was with just giggled and whispered something amongst themselves in true girl fashion. Ricky saw this as his opportunity. He went in for the kill. He approached her, introduced himself and asked her name.

"Hello, how you doing? My name is Ricky. What's your name if you don't mind me asking?"

"No, I don't mind. It's Yuki." (You–Key)

"Yuki huh? That's a beautiful name."

"Thanks."

"So Yuki, what's a brotha gotta do to get to know you better?"

"Well, we can start by exchanging numbers."

"That's wuss up."

They exchanged phone numbers. Ricky promised to give her a call a little later, gently shook her hand and told her, "it was very nice to meet you."

She smiled and said, "likewise."

After meeting Yuki and leaving the mall Ricky was on cloud 9. He knew that if he pulled off turning out Yuki that it'd be like hitting the jackpot. That's when the name came to him. "Jackpot!" He thought about, and said to himself, "that shit's tight!" From then on, Ricky Walters would be known as Jackpot. Jackpot Tha Pimp, JP for short.

JP couldn't wait to get home and call Yuki. He had so much game in his brain to spit that he was ready to burst. He already knew everything he was gonna, and wanted to say. But little did he know that it would not be that easy. See pimpin is a sport, and just like "any" sport you have to master the game. Just because you know the rules to basketball doesn't mean you're gonna be able to slam dunk, and pimpin was no exception. Nine o'clock that night JP gave Yuki a call. "Hello, may I speak to Yuki?"

"Yes, this is she."

"Hi, this is JP."

"Who?"

"Oh Ricky, we met at the mall. Sorry, my friends call me JP."

"Ohh, the cute guy in the food court with the nice smile."

"Yeah that's me." They both laughed.

"So JP, why don't you tell me a little about yourself, other than the fact that you're handsome and have a nice smile?"

Wow, this girl was straight forward and spoke with confidence. Like she knew exactly what she wanted or expected out of life, JP thought to himself. At that moment he knew he was gonna have to bring out his "A" game and stay on point like a #2 pencil. "Well I graduated high school not too long ago. I just quit my job because I didn't see any future in it."

"Really, what was the job?"

"Security, and I have too much ambition to be sitting around playing cop with no gun and a flashlight." They both laughed. "Is that right?" Yuki asked in a sarcastic but playful manner. "So then if that's the case, then tell me about some of your ambitions?" Yuki asked. That caught JP off guard because he couldn't tell her that his ambitions was to become the biggest, richest, and flyest pimp to ever live. Even though that's exactly what they were. Then JP remembered something that Trust had told him. "When it comes to bitches you have to be a chameleon." So he told her his ambitions was to have control of his own destiny and get rich while doing so.

"So how you plan on going about doing that?" Yuki asked. *Shit, this bitch got all the right questions. Who's trying to pimp and game who?* JP thought to himself playfully, then answered the question.

"By putting my best foot forward, marching ahead and not stopping until it reaches the promise land, and that big pot of gold at the end of the rainbow." At this point JP was in Yuki's good ear. She was feeling all his answers to her questions. And the more JP talked, the more she listened. The more she listened, the more intrigued she was with him. She had never heard a man speak about life the way JP did. He was passionate, sincere and knew what he wanted out of life. "Enough about me though, how about yourself?" JP asked.

"Well my life's pretty complicated. My parents moved to the states when I was 3 from Japan." *That explains a lot,* JP thought to himself. "My dad was killed in a car accident when I was 5 by a drunk driver, so I never really got a chance to know him." Usually, Yuki wouldn't speak so freely about her personal life with someone she just met, but there was something different about JP. She didn't know what it was, but something about him just made her feel comfortable opening up. She continued.

"My mother did her best to provide and raise me as a single parent, but it was hard."

"Where's your mom now?"

"She passed away last year due to breast cancer."

"Wow." That really shocked JP and caught him off guard. He wasn't expecting that response. But then as cold as it may sound, he thought...*that's kinda cool. No negative outside influences if I turn her out and she becomes my hoe. No parents, ties or baggage to step in the way and throw a monkey wrench in the program.* "Sorry ta hear that," JP responded. "So who do you live with now, if you don't mind me asking?"

"I live with a friend. I've been on my own since my mother died. All of my family lives in Japan and I've been in America so long I never got a chance to meet, or get to know them."

Ah shit, this is perfect, JP thought to himself, as he mentally thanked the pimp god for blessing him with the perfect bitch. JP and Yuki talked for over 4 hours that night. He didn't rush trying to turn her out because he didn't wanna scare her off. His mother always told him "good things come to those who wait, and patience is a virtue."

So with that thought in mind, he pumped his breaks and put his pimpin in slow motion. He knew it would only be a matter of time, as long as he played all his cards right and didn't rush, that Yuki would be his. The next morning JP woke up an called the flower shop down the block from his old job and had a dozen long stem roses plus 1 "blue" one with a card made up, put together, and sent that said, "there's a dozen sweet things I could say about you but time is of the essence so I'll just use 1...unique!" JP knew that a blue rose was rare. The only reason he knew about it was because his mother loved them so much. After he got off the phone with the florist, he called Yuki to tell her good morning, and that he enjoyed their conversation last night. He then asked if he could pick her up later on and take her out to somewhere nice. She agreed and gave him her address. JP told her that he'll be over to pick her up at 7 p.m. They said their goodbyes, and hung up the phone. JP then called the flower shop back and gave them Yuki's address as to let them know where to send the flowers he ordered earlier, hung up the phone and jumped in the shower.

4 MAKE IT HAPPEN

JP parked the car right in front of the ticket line for the Horn Blower dinner cruise at the San Diego harbor. He still had $900 left over from the money he saved up, and all of that was about to go to prepping Yuki. So JP bought two $75 per person plates and tickets to tonight's Horn Blower dinner yacht cruise.

He knew this this would definitely impress her. The cruise consisted of a 2 hour, 3 floor level, yacht cruise around the bay. You could see the San Diego skyline as well as the legendary Coronado bridge. The cruise had a 5 star dinner on board, a DJ playing top 40, dim lights, and quality champagne.

This was gonna be a night to remember. After JP purchased the tickets, it was a little after 3 p.m. The cruise was at 8 p.m. and he had to pick up Yuki at 7 p.m. So he was good on time as long as everything continued to run smooth and go as clockwork. He then headed to the mens store downtown which was only a few blocks away to get a suit and some Stacy's. Trust told him during their talk that, "if you look like a pimp, you feel like a pimp. So always dress to finesse and set yourself apart from the rest." So with that thought in mind, JP went to buy a suit.

------$$$$------

"Hello, may I help you find anything today?" The oriental lady behind the counter said, with a slight smile and eager look on her face like she was hungry for a sale.

"Yes, I'm looking for a nice suit. Nothing too flashy, but nothing too plain either. Oh yeah, and some nice shoes to match," JP answered. This was JP's first time shopping for a suit, so he really didn't know what he was looking for or had anything set in his mind. The only time he ever wore a suit in the past was to church, and his mother bought those.

"How about this?" the clerk asked as she pointed to a bright red suit with matching tie and fake snake skin shoes. *Hell nah!* JP thought to himself, *that look like some shit straight out of a 1970's pimp movie.* That's when he spotted the perfect suit hanging above his head on the wall. It was a 3 piece suit from the Steve Harvey collection and was on sale for $200. "Yeah, that's perfect," JP said to himself. He went into the dressing room and tried it on after the clerk pulled it down from the wall and handed it to him. "Good choice, you look really handsome in that suit." *Yeah I bet she says that to all the customers,* JP thought to himself. *But she ain't lying this time. I look flyer than a 747.* "Let me find you shirt. You like french cuff or regular?" the clerk asked, with a strong oriental accent. JP didn't know the difference. Shit, this was his first real suit. "Umm, I don't know. What's a french cuff?"

"Those are shirts that use cuff links," said the clerk, hoping he opt for the french cuff shirt because it was more expensive, plus she could sell him some cuff links as well and make even more money on the final sale.

"Oh yeah, I'll take the french cuffs. Those look sharp. Let me check out some of your cuff links too, I'm not really feeling the ones that come with the shirt."

That was music to the store clerks ears. "We have some right here. You pick, I get."

JP looked through the selection when he spotted a pair with the initials "JP." Not only that but it came with a matching tie clip. "Oh hell yeah! that's perfect right there. Let me get those," JP said while pointing at the cuff link set.

"Good choice, good choice!" said the money hungry clerk. Next, JP picked out some nice Stacy Adams, a belt, and a tie with the matching handkerchief and called it a day. The total came out to about $340 which left JP a little over $400 in his stack. JP thought, *more than enough to prep Yuki and still have a little pocket change left over at the end of the night.* After leaving the mens store and arriving home, JP's phone rang. It was Yuki. "Hey wuss up babe, how you doing? I was just thinking about you."

"I'm fine, I just got the flowers you sent. You're so sweet. No one has ever sent me roses before, let alone a 'blue' rose." Yuki was very impressed and happy with her roses JP's thoughtful gesture.

"I'm glad you like em. It was money well spent. Oh yeah, I forgot to tell you, dress to impress tonight. Put on your best evening gown. I'm taking you out somewhere elegant."

"Okay, I can't wait."

"See you at 7. Bye"

"Bye." They both hung up the phone. JP knew he was batting a thousand and had made all the right moves. Now all he had to do was seal the deal. "Tonight will be a night to remember," JP said to himself. And little did he know that, that would be the understatement of the year.

5 PREP TIME

Seven o'clock on the dot, JP arrived at Yuki's house. She lived on Adams Ave in East San Diego, right around the corner and a few blocks from the track. East Diego, more properly pronounced and spelled as East "Daygo," was the ghetto side of San Diego. So was the South East. These were the section and parts of San Diego where the gangsters dwelled. Bloods, crips, pimps, smokers, hustlers, tweekers, you name it, it was there. Due to the fact that JP knew this all too well, he was extra cautious and on point when he arrived, parked, and got out his ride.

Knock knock knock, JP tapped on the door after noticing the door bell was broken. Yuki opened the door and greeted JP with a warm smile and hello. JP smiled, said hello, gave her a nice hug and asked if she was ready to go. She said yes and closed the door. "You look real sexy tonight. I love that dress.

It looks really good on you."

"Thanks, you look handsome in your suit as well. I'm very impressed."

"Well you ain't seen nothing yet babe. This night is all about you. The sky's the limit, and if you look, that's a long way up." JP knew he was on his "A" game with that one. Yuki blushed with a smile and look that said, "really?"

JP offered his arm in a gentlemen like manner. She interlocked her arms with his as they left her house and walked towards the car. JP went to open the passenger side door for Yuki as she said, "nice car."

"Thanks." He opened the door, gently grabbed her hand, and led her into the car. JP smiled and nodded with a devilish grin and got in the car.

"Emmm, your car smells nice."

"Thanks." JP always kept a dozen of tree air fresheners hanging from the turn signal. Every time he got his car washed he would just add new trees but never threw out the old ones. So his car stayed smelling fresh. JP already had all the right music pre-selected and put into the cd changer before he left the house. He had Tupac for the ride up to the harbor and a slow jam mix for the ride back afterwards, to set the mood.

See Trust taught JP that prepping a bitch was like chess. You needed a beginning, a middle, as well as an end game. If one out of them three parts of your game was weak, you could best believe turning out the bitch and making her a successful hoe would be a bust. So JP made sure everything was well thought out and planned from beginning to end, start to finish. He left nothing to chance. Not if he could help it. And so far so good. Everything was going according to plan.

JP jumped on the I-5 freeway and headed towards downtown. He got off on the Harbor drive exit and made his way to the docks. The car ride was quiet, but not that uncomfortable first date silence. Just quiet. They were both enjoying the music and just waiting to get to their destination.

Yuki had no idea what JP had planned and couldn't wait to find out. This was the first time anyone had ever took her on a formal date since prom, and to her that didn't count. That's when she was 17 in her senior year in high school. But as most girls, she grew up fast, and most of the boys her age was not on her level. Their idea of a good date was a movie and sex.

First I take you out to a movie, then you give me sex. Or, let's go meet at the mall and hang out, then afterwards go roller skating? No thanks, you won't be hitting this for a $7 movie ticket and a large popcorn. Yuki was ambitious and always knew the power she had over men. She saw the trick mentality within men early on. Especially one day in the 9th grade when her science teacher Mr Johnson came on to her. She never told anyone. She just used the situation to her advantage by stringing him along all throughout the semester to receive straight A's. All the while not having even slept with him once.

See Yuki wasn't your average female. She wasn't the gullible, let a guy run drag and get you in the sack with a happy meal and a 40 ounce type bitch. See her mom use to work in a massage parlor in Atlanta when she was young, because all the ones in San Diego had got shut down in the 80's when they started cleaning up downtown. So her mom would take weekend trips to Atlanta, work, and be back in Daygo by that following monday. This was how they got by and made ends meet when her father died. So Yuki growing up watching, as well as being laced by her mom about everything from, male manipulation to actual work in the parlor made her sharp. This was also a side of her past that she kept hidden. Even her best friends didn't know. Yuki knew that most people would never understand, or they would pre-judge, point fingers and hate on what they didn't understand. Another fact her mother taught her when she was young. So she always kept that side of her to herself. Little did JP know at the time, that Yuki was born to be a hoe...but he would soon find out.

------$$$$------

"Well we're here babygirl," JP said as they pulled up and parked the car right by the docks. Still not having a clue as to what the night had in store, Yuki looked around puzzled as to say, "so where we going? I don't see any club or restaurant. Just a bunch of boats, and I know we're not going on one of them."

The thought of JP taking Yuki on an elegant dinner cruise never entered her mind. Even while being parked and looking at the huge ships in front of them. JP got out the car, walked around to Yuki's side of the door and opened it.

"Why thank you handsome," said Yuki.

"You're welcome pretty lady." JP closed her door behind her and gently grabbed her hand. *What a gentleman,* Yuki thought to herself. "So where are you taking me this lovely evening?" Yuki asked, with a sexy smile and puppy dog like eyes. Jackpot smiled, while looking Yuki in the eyes and said...

"Right here. Just look up. Your chariot awaits." JP pointed at the Horn Blower yacht. Yuki couldn't believe it. She had never been on a boat before let alone a yacht. Especially on a date. This was by far, beyond her expectations. JP knew by the excited look on Yuki's face that he had made the right decision.

"Come my queen." They walked along to get on the boat.

"Say cheese! *(click flash!)* one of the crew members said as they snapped a picture of JP and Yuki getting on the boat as a souvenir. "You can view and purchase copies of this picture later if you like it after the cruise," said the photographer.

"Thanks, will do," JP responded back, as they got on the boat and took it all in. Now truth be told, this was JP's first time on a boat as well. So he was just as excited and taken back by the yacht, and how elegant it was as Yuki. But he kept his feelings inside to give off a, "this is how we do it when you fuck wit JP" impression to Yuki. And truth be told, it was working. The date had just started and she was already feeling like this was the best date of her life. "Would you like to be seated at your table?" the waitress asked.

"Yes please," JP said with a smile.

"We have a nice table over here with a great view overlooking the water."

"That'll be perfect." They walked to their table, look and feeling like royalty. After being seated, the waitress asked if they would like to start off with a bottle of champagne? JP said yes, they would like a bottle of Moet and chocolate covered strawberries. *Wow!* Yuki thought to herself, *I'm impressed. Usually a guy just wanna buy shots of Hennesey in hopes of getting a bitch drunk enough to give him some pussy at the end of the night. And even if he did have enough class to get the Moet, it was never with a chocolate covered chaser. That's the kind of shit you see in the movies.*

While they waited for the waitress to come back with their champagne and strawberries, the boat finished loading up the remaining passengers so they could leave the dock. While doing so, JP and Yuki enjoyed the soft R&B tunes played by the house DJ for the evening. JP thought to himself, *this shit really sets the mood. By the end of the night, if I continue to play my cards right, I should have this bitch turned out like some dirty laundry.*

The waitress returned to the table with their champagne and strawberries, corked the bottle, smiled, and then left them to be alone. JP poured a glass for them both and made a toast. "To a night we both shall never forget." Yuki agreed and toasted to the occasion. They both took a sip from their glasses followed by a bite of the chocolate covered strawberries, which JP fed to Yuki personally. At that moment, the ship began to exit the dock and get on its way for the cruise. "You know I never been on a boat before, especially one as nice as this."

"Really? Well there's a first time for everything and I'm just honored to be the first to make it happen for you." Yuki smiled at JP's response with a slight blush. After about 15 minutes into the cruise and 3 glasses of champagne later, the waitress returned. "May I start you guys off with your appetizer for the evening?"

"Yes, that'll be fine," said JP. The appetizer for the evening was spinach and artichoke dip with salt water crackers. The appetizer they ordered arrived almost instantly. "Wow, what great service," said Yuki. "That was pretty quick"

"Only the best for my princess," JP said as they both smiled like he had something to do with the dish coming out as fast as it did. At that moment, the inside lights on the boat got very dim and all you could see was the elegant candle lights that sat on the tables. 20 minutes later the waitress brought out their main course. A nice tender well cut steak cooked to perfection in bourbon sauce, mixed vegetables, and risotto with fresh baked dinner rolls hot out the oven. For dessert, they had a flambe, which the waitress lit on fire right at their table. Yuki knew at "that" moment that she would never forget this night.

After dinner was over, JP ordered another bottle of Moet, poured a glass for them both, and asked Yuki if she would like to have their drinks on the top deck. She said yes and grabbed her glass as JP led her by the hand upstairs. As they arrived to the top section of the deck, the cool ocean breeze from the San Diego night air filled the atmosphere.

"Ooh, it's nice out here," said Yuki.

"Yeah, just about as nice as you look in that dress," JP responded, with a playful but serious laugh. As they walked to the front of the ship arm and arm, they took in the lovely view of the San Diego skyline as the ship began to go under the Coronado bridge. As they were going under, a crew member told em, "legend has it that, if you kiss while going under the Coronado bridge your relationship will last seven more years." *Ah, good looking out G. What better opportunity and good excuse to have our first kiss?* JP thought to himself. So just before they were almost completely passed the bridge, JP turned, looked Yuki dead in her eyes with a sensual glare. Gently pulled her close, and gave her a passionate kiss. Yuki closed her eyes as his tongue entered her mouth ever so gently. It wasn't the wet over the top sloppy, awkward, first date kiss either. But more of a sensual, short, straight to the point, can't wait to finish where we left off later kind of kiss...and she loved every second of it.

After the kiss, JP stroked the side of her face with the back of his hand and gave her a soft peck on the lips. *Mission complete.* JP was making "all" the right moves. Yuki was like putty in his hands. "Would you like to go back downstairs and dance? JP asked.

"Sure, I'd love too." They headed back downstairs to the lower deck. The DJ was playing a slow song by R-Kelly. "Oh that's my jam," said Yuki as she grabbed JP's hand and took the lead towards the dance floor. JP took off the top half of his suit, stripping down to the vest, placed it on the back of his chair near their table and got back on the dance floor where Yuki was already semi grooving to the music, swaying back and fourth side to side with her hands up in the air snapping her fingers to the beat.

JP joined Yuki. All eyes was on them, like they were a prince and princess dancing the first song of the evening. They truly stood out. People was coming by them all night just to say how wonderful of a couple they were. *If only they knew that this was just our first date*, JP and Yuki thought secretly to themselves.

"Thanks!" Yuki responded as the last person of the evening told them for the unteenth time that they both looked good together and made a great couple. "See, a thousand people can't be wrong. It is what it is. I guess it's safe to say that we was meant to be together," said JP. Yuki just smiled with a look of agreement as she placed the side of her head on JP's chest and slow danced the last song of the evening. She wished this night would last forever, but it wouldn't. And little did she know that after tonight, her life as she knew it would dramatically change forever.

Back at Yuki's House

"JP, I don't want this night to end. It's been so wonderful. I never met a guy like you before. I don't want you to leave or go home. I want to spend the night with you." *Hell yeah!* JP thought to himself. That was the only thing left he needed to do to lock this bitch down. And now she was giving him the green light and pussy on a silver platter. Trust had told him that, you gotta make a bitch fall in love with you, and if it's too early for that, then she has to at least be able to see herself with, and picture falling in love with you one day or sometime in the future.

JP knew that after laying his dick game down tight, she'd be his for sure. So he downplayed the situation, not trying to look or come across too eager. "You sure baby? I don't wanna rush into anything you might not be ready for. As much as I wanna be with you in every way imaginable, I'm willing to put my wants and feelings aside until you're truly ready and want me the same way. That way, in the morning when we both wake up in each others arms, you'll have no regrets." *Damn I'm good,* JP thought to himself. By him saying that, it just made Yuki want him more.

"I know what I want, and I know where I want to be...it's with you," Yuki said to JP with a sincere look in her eyes.

"Okay, then let me take you somewhere special. Come with me Babygirl." They left Yuki's house, jumped back in the car and headed off.

"Where are we going babe?"

"It's a surprise," JP said as they rode down the freeway, then merged onto the coronado bridge. The coronado bridge was unique because it's one of the only bridges that elevate and turn at an angle. As they descended and came towards the end of the bridge, they passed a toll and crossed over into coronado. JP knew about a spot in coronado that overlooked the San Diego skyline that sat right over the water. It was actually the same waters they had just cruised not even hours before. There, sat a nice 5 star hotel resort with actual real pink flamingos walking out front and the whole nine yards. As they pulled up to the valet, JP turned to Yuki and said, "I brung you here, because those waters you see in front of us is where we started our date, or should I say...adventure. So if you don't mind, overlooking those same waters is where I'd like to continue it." Yuki couldn't believe how thoughtful, sweet and caring JP was. If there was ever any doubt in her mind about tonight, which there wasn't, this very last gesture of JP's erased it completely. She was ready to give her all to him. As the valet gave them a claim ticket and parked their car, they headed towards the front desk. "Hello, may I help you Sir?"

"Yes, I would like one of your finest rooms with a view overlooking the coast and San Diego skyline."

"Not a problem Sir, let me get that for you." The night manager started typing on his computer to see what type of rooms they had available. "Will that be smoking or non-smoking?" asked the clerk.

"Non."

"Okay, I have a non-smoking mini suite with a hot tub and king size bed overlooking the water."

"That's perfect, we'll take it," said JP. The night manager smiled and said, "will that be cash or credit?"

"Cash."

"Okay, that's $200 a night and checkout is at noon. If you need anything dial 0-9 on your room phone and it'll get you the front desk. Dial 0-8 and it'll get you room service."

"Thank you," said JP eager to get upstairs to their room while trying not to let it show.

"Here's your room keys." JP payed the clerk, grabbed the keys, and headed for their room. By this time JP was broke. He had spent damn near his last on the room. $900 gone. But he was okay with it because he knew by the morning...Yuki would be turned out!

6 FRE$H TURNOUT

Wow, that was amazing, Yuki thought to herself while laying in JP's arms, after experiencing the best sex she ever had in her life. They made love for 3 hours straight, all over the hotel room. From the bed to the jacuzzi, back to the bed, in the shower, on the bathroom counter, pretty much touching everything up in the hotel room.

At this point JP knew he was in there. Now was the best time to seal the situation. Go hard or go home, and JP had spent too much dough on the bitch to go home. It was now or never.

"Hey Babygirl, can we rap a taste for a second?"

"Sure Daddy, what's on your mind?" Yuki responded, still naked in bed looking up at JP.

"Well, I want to start off by saying that, I've never met a girl like you in my life, and even though we just met, I feel like we click in a way that most couples can only dream of, and here it is only our

1st date. I also feel like everything happens for a reason and fate brought us together because nothing in life just happens by chance."

"I agree. It's funny you should say that because I was actually thinking the same thing. It's like you're in my mind or something. Like, just as I was thinking that, you said it." *Well lets hope this bitch is thinking bout choosing up and hoe'n because that's where this conversation is going,* thought JP, as he continued to speak. "See that's what I'm saying. Babygirl I have dreams. But more so than that, I have ambition, and with ambition you can make dreams come true. Even better if you have the right woman by your side down to ride to the very end. That shit's like the perfect sundae wit a cherry on top. What would Clyde have been without Bonnie? Would they be as famous today if they were apart back then? Probably not. But 2 is always better than 1, put both minds together and you get shit done."

"So what are you saying Daddy?"

"If you let me finish I'll tell you. I feel like you contain the same type of qualities as me which is far from a squares mind frame and way of thinking. I feel like you have that rare quality to grab life by the nuts and make shit happen. See I don't believe that everything you see is just black & white. We live in a color high definition complexed world. So one must think outside the box and separate ourselves from the rest. The unfortunate part about that is, our planet is made up of mostly squares and haters who push their laws on society with their, in the box way of thinking like they're god. Then when a intellectual like myself challenges those laws and ways of thinking, they wanna throw me in jail or say that I'm committing the ultimate sin. See this is just some of the things that be on my mind but really I can get a lot deeper than that, and if I did we'd be here all day and night. We live in a society that feels they can dictate how one should live, what you can and can't do within your own home. Who you can and can't marry. What a woman can and can't do with her own body. What is and isn't gonna bring you closer to god. All the while little preacher man is touching on 10 year old Johnny, while the president is getting his dick sucked in the white house by his secretary.

"Black and poor people are struggling in the hood wit minimal help from our government. The same government that'll lock you up for stealing but then steal an election. I mean this is the world we live in Babygirl. So I can't just sit back and play follow the leader like a fuckin puppet. We live in a world where only the strong survive. The rich get richer and rule the planet, while the poor gets poorer and left out of the american dream. This is our reality.

"Life is what you make it. You can play the game straight as an arrow but chances are you won't get far, and hitting a bulls eye is very slim to none." JP was in a zone. He kept spitting about everything from mankind to how our country was built on corruption. "Don't get it twisted Babygirl, we didn't become the richest and most powerful country in the world by playing the game fair. Oh no, no, no...never that." Yuki was stuck on JP's every word. She had never heard anyone talk or view life in the way he did, and it wasn't just talk, it was true. She had always felt the same way about a lot of the things JP was speaking about, but JP was taking it to a whole nother level. Expanding her mind and way of thinking to a much broader picture. How could she not feel what he was saying, it was true. JP continued talking while she just listened and took it all in. She didn't want him to stop. She wanted to hear more.

"See Babygirl, people judge what they don't understand. They point fingers like they're not human themselves and can do no wrong, but then behind closed doors where they feel no one can see be on some other shit. Like a judge that may rule against same sex marriage, but be cross dressing and trying on women's clothing at home. Or the cop that arrest you for domestic violence, get off work, go home, and beats on his wife because the job has him stressed out.

"I tell you babygirl there's a thin line between right and wrong, which is why politicians break the very same laws they create everyday. With all this being said, I live by my own rules and that's, if at the end of the day it makes me happy and I'm not hurting or bringing any harm to anyone else in the process, then it's all good and fuck what society has to say about it. Society is built of mostly haters. People hate you because they ain't you. Hate you for your style, hate you for your smile. Hate you for your good relationship because theirs is bad. Hate you because you have money and they don't. Just a bunch of hate, hate, hate, hate, hate!

"But I'll tell you this about me. You could drop me from a 10 story building and not one hater bone a come out my body when I hit the ground. See I'm a congratulator not a hater. When I see someone doing good or better than me, it just gives me motivation to do good or better for myself. Step my game up. And when I look for a woman, I look for one with the same or similar qualities as myself. She gotta be money motivated and goal orientated. Head screwed on tight and knows what she wants outta life. I'm looking for a 10 which is more than her looks but, mind body and soul. Romeo and Juliet willing to die for each other, but at the same time, ain't afraid to set it off for the dough like Queen Latifa. Babygirl, for the first time in my life I feel like I may have found that woman."

Yuki couldn't believe what she was hearing because she definitely felt the same about JP. She also felt like she was, "that" woman. She was stuck on JP's every word. She had never met a man like him before. If there was such a thing as love at first sight, then this was it. "So what's the next step Daddy?" Yuki asked, then continued. "Cause I'm definitely feeling you and everything you're saying."

"The next step is to get money. Ta chase that big pot of gold at the end of the rainbow, and believe me, it's there. Are you down to do whatever it takes to get this money Babygirl?"

"What do you mean daddy?"

"Just what I said. Are you willing to do what it takes by any means necessary?"

"Yes daddy, as long as you have my back and is right there by my side."

"Well Babygirl, you never have to worry bout that. As long as we're together I'll always be by your side."

"So what do you want me to do Daddy?"

"I'm gonna introduce you to the life. The world of pimpin and hoe'n. Now I know when you hear that, the first thang that comes to mind is some man in a flashy clown suit, beating on you and taking your money. Well lets do away with that stereotype and misconception from the gate. TV, books, and society gave true pimps a bad rap and the game a black eye. They want you to believe that a pimp is the scum of the earth. That he doesn't respect women, even if that woman is his own mother. That he beats and rape women for control. All of these allegations are false. A true pimp loves and respects his mother to the fullest. A true pimp doesn't have to force a bitch to do shit because he's well aware that the game is about choice.

"Either a bitch choose to be with a pimp or she doesn't. A true pimp would never rape a bitch for the pussy because he's not a trick. He's in the business of selling pussy not taking it. A true pimp 'does' care about his hoes because without them, they'd be no him. A true pimp doesn't beat on his bitches with his fist but his lips, because he's promoting prostitution not boxing.

"Now don't get me wrong Babygirl, you have some fake ass wannabe no game having gorilla pimpatraters out there, breaking all these rules in the name of pimpin. But let me assure you Babygirl, that's what it's not! I also don't condone or believe in pimpin on minors. This is a grown mans game so I'm looking for grown women on my team. 17 and younger need not apply.

"I truly feel like you have what it takes to be a star, and with the right guidance and man in your corner, can't nothing hold you back. Now a lot of haters would say you're dumb and why pay a pimp when you can pay yourself? Well let me answer that for you. First of all, I'm not a fake person so I'm a keep it real with you at all times. I'm not gonna say you 'need' a pimp, and you can't do this by yourself. Of course you can. It's not even about that. It's about 2 like minded individuals down wit one another, getting it in a real way and taking over the world together. It's about being wit someone who won't judge you. Someone who'll let you be yourself without throwing it back in your face when times get rough. Bonnie and Clyde could have robbed banks alone, but they came up faster together. What type a man can truly be with a hoe without getting jealous or seeing something wrong wit it other than a pimp? There is none. Even a hoe needs companionship. Also, it's in a bitches nature to spend money. She gets paid on friday, go get her hair and nails done, new outfit, and is broke by monday. Wit a pimp, he gon make sure he stack the money every night.

"He gon do without in the beginning so they can ball in the end. Not to mention, if a hoe was to ever get locked up, who she gonna call to bail her out? Not her momma or square ass friends.

"So you see Babygirl that's what it's all about. A lot of bitches hate on hoes but be tramping at the club every weekend. See a hoe gets paid but a tramp fucks for free. I have no respect for a tramp. A tramp a fuck the milk man, mail man, and the pool boy all in the same week with nothing to show for it but, a worn out loose pussy and notch on the mens belt afterwards. They don't respect her either.

"But a hoe doesn't put herself out there like that. She has class. She'll never fuck for free unless it's her folks. She knows the value of her pussy and it's worth. So all the while them square bitches is hating on hoes, little do they know they're doing the same thang for a #4 at McDonald's and a ride home from the club. Real shit! They're hoe'n as well, just for a lot less."

At this point Yuki was lost for words. She didn't know what to say. Not because she was offended or didn't like JP's proposition, but more because of how real he spoke and put the entire game in perspective. He made you analyze and view the game in a different light, and truth be told, giving Yuki's background, mother, and up bringing, she never really saw anything wrong with hoe'n. Shit her momma did it. She just could never see herself with a pimp...until now. "So if I said yes and chose ta be with you in that way, you'd take care of me?" asked Yuki with a sincere look in her eyes.

"No Babygirl, we'd take care of each other." *Good answer,* Yuki thought to herself, but at the same time she couldn't help but feel like it might be all game. Still being, she felt she didn't have much to lose. If it all turned out to be a bunch of game and JP done the direct opposite of what he preached, all she had to do was leave him. Yeah it might hurt once she caught major feelings, but she knew she could do it.

Remember, she thought to herself, *momma didn't raise no square.* And as passionate, caring, and loving Yuki was, one thing she didn't do was wear her heart on her sleeve. But then again, she never had a man like JP before either. Yuki agreed to give hoe'n a try which was music to JP's ears. He had played all of his cards right and was dealt a winning hand. By the time JP was done prepping Yuki about all the ends and outs and rules of the game, it was a new day. Checkout time was in an hour.

7 BREAKIN LUCK

The Birth Of Jackpot

"Hey Babygirl I'm outside."

"Okay daddy, I'll be out in a second." As Yuki hung up the phone, she took one last look in the mirror to make sure she looked alright. After which, she grabbed her purse, fixed a piece of hair that was out of place, and left the house. Today would be the day that Yuki's life changed forever.

"Hey Daddy!" Yuki said, as she got in the car and kissed JP on the cheek.

"Hey Babygirl, damn you looking hotter than a summers day in july." Yuki had on a school girl skirt. The type you see some girls wearing in porn movies. Real short, red and black checkered plaid, 6 inch clear bottom hoe shoes with a sexy shirt that pushed up her C cup titties to look like D's, revealing her perfectly flat stomach and sexy belly button piercing.

"You look like a million bucks."

Yuki just smiled and said, "You gotta look like a million if you plan on attracting a million. Ain't that what you told me daddy?"

"Hell yeah. Shit, good to see you was listening," Jackpot said as they both laughed and drove off headed to the hoe stroll also known as the track. In later years it would come to be known as the blade. Whatever you chose to call it, this was where a bitch walked the streets and made money. On the way to the track, Jackpot laced Yuki to some basic rules to keep her safe while on the stroll.

"Babygirl, I need you to listen up and listen close," Jackpot said, as he turned down the bass in his ride and got Yuki's undivided attention. "When you out there on the track you have yo be on your P's and Q's at all times. Remember, it's a dog eat dog world out there on them streets. Don't get caught up Ho'cializing. Which is basically standing around gossiping wit other hoes on the track. Only fuck wit white tricks because they're the ones wit money. Never and I repeat...**NEVER!** fuck wit blacks and mexicans. Reason being, mexicans are cheap and blacks wanna get their money's worth. Be tryna hit the pussy all night like you his girlfriend leaving you sore and stretched out by the end of the date.

"Not only that, but he might be a pimp, which brings me to this. If you're ever in the presence of another pimp, put your head down and walk the other way. Never look another pimp in his eyes because if you do, then he's gonna get the impression that you're interested in his pimpin and tryna choose up, at which time, you will be deemed outta pocket and subject ta be put under pimp arrest. That's when he can break you for everything you have and own. So never put yourself in that position. If someone ask you who's your folks? You tell em Jackpot, JP Tha Pimp! If you see a unhappy hoe, you try and pull her and bring her home, Because we're tryna make our stable grow. You understand Babygirl?"

"Yes daddy." Jackpot got off on the National City 8th Street exit and pulled into the gas station. He went inside and bought Yuki a box of condoms. "Listen up Babygirl" Jackpot held up the box and continued speaking. "Never do anything without a condom and that means, nothing! I don't care if it's a mutha fuckin hand job, you put a condom on. And if the mutha fucka's dick look too big you put on 2."

"Okay Daddy." Jackpot handed Yuki the box of condoms, started the car, and drove onto the track. At first glance the track looked like a ghost town. *Damn, where the hoes at?* Jackpot thought to himself. If it wasn't for all the cars rolling down this side street with curious looking male figures behind the wheel, he would have swore he had the wrong track. Just at that moment he saw a hooker get out of a tricks car up the street. Then another, and another. Then he saw a couple of pimps dropping off their hoes. In no time the track was looking like grand central station.

Jackpot dropped Yuki off in front of the Trophy Lounge night club and had her walk up the street to the track. Before she left he gave her a pager and said, "If I hit you up wit 1602, it means to meet me back here. If you need me for something, hit me on mines with the code 304. If it's an emergency, 304*911."

"Okay Daddy, thanks for the pager." Yuki kissed her folks on the cheek and walked to the track.

Okay 12:35, It's still early, JP thought to himself, while glancing at his watch. *I'll post up on the track and keep an eye on Yuki to see how she doing,* Jackpot continued to think to himself, as he rode down the track and parked on the side of the hotel near a fire hydrant, where he posted up and sat low key.

By this time the track was booming. Everywhere you looked there was hoes in skanky outfits, barely dressed and getting money. Some of the bitches looked like crack whores. A lot were bad, but no one looked better than Yuki. And the fact that she never stayed on the corner more than 5 minutes without being picked up by a trick proved as much.

A lot of the black hoes on the track saw this and you could see the envy and hate in their eyes, but what could they do? Yuki was a rare breed on the track. A real hot commodity. Shit, of course they couldn't compete. There were over a dozen black bitches out there, in all shapes and sizes. There was even a few snow bunnies. But there was only 1 asian...and that was Yuki.

So the moment Yuki stepped foot on the track, she had the shit sold up! Other pimps saw this too and tried to push up on her between dates, but Yuki just did as she was told. Put her head down, didn't make eye contact, and walked the opposite direction. For the most part it was working, until one player decided to grab her by the arm to finish talking to her and get his point across. Jackpot saw this and figured it was time for him to take action and say something. So he got out the car and approached the pimp to assess the situation.

"Hey wuss up pimpin? That's my bitch you got there by the arm. Now I know the hoe ain't outta pocket because I been watching her like a hawk in the sky at a fox. Now we promoting pimpin around here not violence. So say what you gotta say ta the bitch, if she ain't tryna hear you, then let her work."

"Ah it ain't like dat pimpin, I feel you. Allow me to properly introduce myself. My name is California Mike."

"Wut up playa? They call me Jackpot, JP Tha Pimp. Daygos finest." They shook hands and chopped it up a bit, while Yuki got back to work. Before she did, she broke herself for $200. "Good job Babygirl. Now keep it up and do what you do best while I handle the rest." Jackpot playfully tapped her on the ass. Yuki smiled and went back to work. While Jackpot and California Mike pimp talked about the game, another pimp was dropping off two of his hoes. It was a pimp name Big Boo. Some called him Boo-J. Boo was a O.G. from 4/7 Neighborhood Crips, but never brought gang banging to the track.

He was about his money and kept it pimpin at all times. He had a cool little stable, but 1 bitch in particular stood out from the rest. She was badder than a mutha fucka! The bitch was light bright and almost white as Pimpin Ken would put it. Long hair, sexy bone structure, and stood about 5'10. 6 foot easy with heels on. This bitch looked like a model. I don't know if she was mixed or not, but I do know that she was the only black or mixed bitch on the track getting it like a white girl. And now at this very moment, Boo-J was dropping her off, along with his bottom. His bottom bitch looked like a smoker but was loyal and knew how to get it. She was a real go getta. What she lacked in looks she made up for in skills. The bitch knew how to trick a john out of his loot. From fake fucking to hollow sucking, the hoe was a pro. Her main skill was robbing tricks. She'd have a trick's dick in one hand and his wallet in another. The bitch was good, and due to the fact, the hoe never came in at night without her quota. "Damn that redbone bitch is bad than a mutha fucka!" Jackpot stated, talking to California Mike while eyeing the hoe.

"Yeah, tell me about it. I've been tryna knock dat bitch since the first night Boo-J set her down."

"Is she new to the game, how long she been hoe'n?" Jackpot asked, with a devilish one eyebrow raised look on his face like he was plotting something."

"Shit, about 2 months. Go ahead and put your bid in pimpin. I already did but the bitch ain't tryna fuck wit me," California Mike stated. *Nah, I'm ah wait till I got my shit together. Wait till I'm in position like a quarter back then, touch down!* Jackpot thought to himself. Just at that moment, Boo-J's bitch, the one that they was talking about, jumped in a tricks car and drove off to pull her date. At the same time she was pulling off, Yuki was stepping out of a tricks car getting dropped back off from finishing her date.

"Alright pimpin, I'll rap a taste with you later. It's always a treat when pimps meet, but I gotta get back to this bitch you dig? Gotta go break this hoe and check my loot," Jackpot said to California Mike.

"Fa'sho, always glad to meet a young up and coming pimp," Mike said as they turned and went back to their business for the day...Pimping!

"Hey Daddy," Yuki said, smiling as she kissed her folks on the cheek.

"Hey Babygirl, wut choo got foe me?"

Yuki pulled out another bankroll, this time totaling $350. The bitch was on a roll, and it had only been a little over an hour since she broke luck. *I knew this bitch was gonna be a star,* Jackpot thought to himself as he counted the money and put it in his pocket. "Good job babygirl. Stay down so we can come up. In a few hours we'll go to keith's restaurant so we can get something to eat."

Keith's was right off the track and stayed open 24 hours. So a lot of pimps and hoes would eat there after a long night of working, putting it down, pimpin, breaking hoes, and checking traps. It was also a good cover to get off the track quickly when the vice was rolling. "Babygirl, I'll be around. If you don't see me but need me, then hit me on the hip."

"Okay daddy." No sooner than Yuki walked off, a trick had stopped, pulled over and picked her up. Since this was Yuki's first day on the track, Jackpot watched her from a far and let his presence be known so she'd feel more comfortable, but little did he know, Yuki was like a pig in shit. It was like she was born to hoe. She was 100% comfortable and took to the game real fast. The more she worked, the more money she made. The more money she made, the more she worked. It was like a new found drug, money being the high and Yuki was addicted.

8 COMING UP

"Check out is at noon. Here are your room keys," the desk clerk said as he handed the hotel keys to Jackpot. "Come on Babygirl. We're in room 304, must be fate," Jackpot said to Yuki, as they both laughed and headed upstairs of the Holiday INN to their room. The reason Jackpot gave Yuki 304 as her secret code to page him was because, "304" spelled hoE upside down.

Yuki jumped in the shower to wash the trick smell off, that all hoes had after a hard days work. As Yuki showered, Jackpot counted the money she made from the days earnings. "$720...40...60... $800. Hell yeah!" Jackpot said to himself. *Not bad for a 1st days work.* He had nearly made back all the money he had invested in prepping Yuki. A veteran hoe was lucky if she even made $500 on that track. And here it was, Yuki's first day out and she made $800. $200 shy of $1000. Jackpot sat back and thought to himself as Yuki finished up and got out the shower. Jackpot placed the money on the night stand where Yuki could see it and said, "this is what it's all about. This is what a little hard work gets you. Feel that, count dat! That's $800 in 8 hours, in 1 day. Shit, the president don't even make money like that. I'm proud of you Babygirl."

"Thanks Daddy." Yuki smiled with excitement. She had never made so much money in one day, in her life. At that very moment they both knew that they were headed for bigger and better things. This was just the beginning. And what a way to start.

------$$$$------

The next morning, Yuki awoke in Jackpot's arms. "Good morning Babygirl, you sleep good?"

"Yes daddy, very good," Yuki answered with a smile and slight morning breath.

"Go brush your teeth and shower up Babygirl, we got a big day ahead of us."

"Okay Daddy. Would you care to join me in the shower?" Yuki said as she got out of bed looking sexier than a model in Penthouse, and feeling freakier than a female in porn.

"Fa'sho, go get the shower ready and I'll be there in a sec, just gotta take a piss," Jackpot responded, as he relieved his morning hard on, then got in the shower and fucked the shit out of Yuki. After they got out of the shower, dried off, and put their clothes on, they headed for the streets.

"Daddy, can we get something to eat please, I'm hungry?"

"Wut choo feel like eating?

"Chinese."

"Alright, I know a good All-You-Can-Eat spot on Plaza."

"Sounds good," Yuki responded, as they headed to the restaurant. After sleeping through breakfast and eating lunch, Jackpot took Yuki to Plaza Bonita for new clothes and Fam-Mart for hoe shoes. Fam-Mart was the local indoor swap meet in the hood. A one stop shop for everything. From CD's and mixtapes to bootleg fashion. You name it, it was there. And if you was on a budget but still wanted to look fly, that's where you'd go.

Every hood in america has a place like this. Ran by mostly asians, and every thing's negotiable. After picking up a brand new pair of hoe shoes that was 1/2 the price of the retail value, Jackpot bought a Too Short CD, as well as a new CD from a local up an coming artist from Daygo name Big June. A lot of underground artist sold their CD's out the trunk in Fam-Mart's parking lot. It's how a lot of San Diego rap legends got started.

After Jackpot bought the shoes and new outfit, he had a little over $600 left. It was 2:20 p.m. and time to get money. There were 2 major tracks in Daygo. The one they worked the day before, 8th St in National City, and El Cajon Blvd. Which was not too far from where Yuki lived. Since they did so well on 8th Street, Jackpot thought...*if it ain't broke, then why fix it?* and took her back to the money track. Before letting Yuki out to work, Jackpot put her up on some more game. "Okay Babygirl check it out. Today is tuesday and that means vice is gonna be out. Every tuesday and thursday is when they work. All across the country on every track in America you can rest assure, that those 2 days, the vice is out like the sun is bright and the night is dark. So be on your toes and extra sharp like a block of cheese.

"Don't take anything for granted or leave nothing to chance. Make a trick pull out his dick or rub on your tits before negotiating anything. Always ask for donations, not money. The rest you already know, okay Babygirl?"

"Yes Daddy, I know wuss up. You don't have to worry about me. I'll be fine. You taught me well, and best believe I was listening."

"Well you know I gotta make sure my bitch is well informed and straight at all times."

"I know, and I appreciate that Daddy. You always have my best interest at heart."

"No doubt. Now get to work Babygirl and get this money. You made $800 yesterday, lets shoot for a G-ball today."

"Okay Daddy, I'll do my best." Jackpot grabbed a box of condoms out the glove box and gave them to Yuki as she got out the car and went to work.

------$$$$------

Man, I'm a go see what some of these other hoes out here is talking bout. See if a pimp can get chosed out in this mutha fucka! Jackpot thought to himself. So while Yuki worked, Jackpot was out on the prowl like a hungry lion searching for his prey. Jackpot rolled up and down the track when he spotted a young snow bunny, bad as a mutha fucka, hopping out of a tricks car from just finishing up a date. Jackpot quickly parked, hopped out the ride, and popped his P's at her. "Hey bitch, wut it do? Dis Jackpot. JP Tha Pimp. Daygo's finest and royal heinous. Not the S.D.P.D but the P.I.M.P. You see I'm desperately seeking Susan for a choosen. Wit me it's all win and no losing. I see you sneaking a peaking but ain't speaking. Study long, study right cause you can best believe the pimpin's air tight and outta sight." The bitch put her head down and ran across the street, but Jackpot didn't mind because it was his first time popping at a hoe and he was on fire.

"Yeah bitch, get your ass across the street. Skip ta my lou and do wut it do, and when you're ready to make that move remember, 619-555-P.I.M.P to reach JP bitch! At that moment, a trick pulled over and picked the hoe up. Jackpot felt energized and ready to mack on everything moving. He couldn't believe how that shit just flowed out his mouth like water. No pre-scripted material. All from the brain. He was a natural, and the more he spit at these hoes, the better he got. The better he got, the more he spit at them.

The game was creating a monster, and his name was Jackpot. At that point, Jackpot set out to be the biggest, most notorious, cross country pimp in history. But in order to do that, he had to get out of Daygo. He had to hit that highway and every track along the way. This was how a pimp got known. Jackpot made it his business to play the game hard. If he wanted to be the best, he knew he had to eat, sleep, shit pimpin 24/7 and be nothing like the rest. 365 he had to keep the pimpin live. There was no off days or breaks. He would tell Yuki, "if you wanted an off day you should have been a secretary, and if you wanted a break a mutha fuckin school teacher.

------$$$$------

4 weeks had passed and Jackpot was getting cold with the pimpin. He stopped calling Yuki Babygirl and started calling her bitch instead. Not to be disrespectful, but to keep the pimpin in her brain at all times, and to never get the situation twisted with some square shit.

Yuki was hitting the track hard, and the money she made every night proved as such. She never came in with less than $500. Most of the time she made $700 or better. She still had yet to make a "G", but that was because 8th Street and El Cajon Blvd. wasn't a $1000 track. She was lucky she was making as much as she was.

"Hey bitch, wuss going on out here?" Jackpot asked Yuki, sitting on the track in his car with the motor idling.

"Nothing much Daddy, it's slow as hell."

"How much you got so far?"

"Like $250, maybe a little less because I had to buy some condoms."

"What! $250, bitch you been out here like 4 hours."

"I know Daddy, but it's slow, the end of the month, and vice is rollin heavy."

"Is dat right? Well then you're gonna have to hoe around them then."

"I know Daddy, that's what I've been doing. They already busted a couple bitches and 3 tricks, so it made the spot kinda hot."*Damn!* "Alright bitch, get in the car. We gon take a ride to Oceanside and see what type a money we can get out there."

"Okay Daddy." Yuki got in the car. Jackpot drove off and got on the I-5 freeway and headed for Oceanside. Oceanside was 45 minutes out of San Diego. A lot of navy men, otherwise known as swabbies lived there. And like San Diego, swabbies were the biggest tricks. The track in Oceanside was right by the beach near the Greyhound bus station. In the 90's, vice hadn't caught on yet, which left the track wide open. You could get some serious dough or pimp at and knock a fine ass hoe without the cops fucking with you. Only thing you had to watch out for was the few transvestite hoes that worked the same track. One night Jackpot was pimpin at a hoe and getting action from afar. The bitch was acting like she was gonna choose up, until she walked up towards the car and turned out to be a man. Jackpot almost fucked the nigga up.

By the time Jackpot and Yuki arrived in Oceanside it was 10:00 p.m. The track was still active and hoes was getting money. Jackpot dropped Yuki off down the street from the Greyhound bus station and had her walk to the track which was right up the block. "Alright bitch, your quota is $700. You already made $200, which means all you need is 5 more so it shouldn't be a problem. After you make your quota, hit me on the pager and I'll come pick you back up here."

"Okay Daddy." Yuki kissed her folks on the cheek and went to make his money. While Yuki went to work, Jackpot hit the track, rolling up and down the strip in his 510 wagon bumping Too Shorts "Cocktales," looking for a new hoe to knock and add to his stable.

The night was coming to a close. 3 hours had passed and Yuki was paging her folks. *Ah, that's the bitch right there,* Jackpot said to himself as he got in his car and left the track to go pick up Yuki.

304*700 was on the pager which meant the bitch had made her quota. The thought of Yuki putting $500 in his hands when he picked her up had Jackpot excited like a kid on christmas. Jackpot arrived at the designated pick up spot 15 minutes after the page. At first glance he couldn't see Yuki, who was chilling in the cut out of sight from watchful eyes waiting for her folks. At second glance he spotted her in the distance walking towards the car.

"Hi Daddy," Yuki said smiling with that proud feeling that all hoes have after a good nights work.

"Hey Babe." Every now and then Jackpot would still call Yuki Babygirl or Babe, especially around squares. He knew that it was a time and place for everything, and sometimes you had to put the pimpin on pause. Yuki reached in her bra and pulled out a big fat bankroll. "I see it was a good night," Jackpot said, counting out the money Yuki just made and handed him. "Yes it was Daddy, I'm glad you brung me up here."

"Fa'sho, you know Daddy always knows best."

"Yes you do, and that's why I listen to you."

"I knew you was probably hungry Babe, so I took the liberty of getting you some food before all the stores closed." Jackpot handed Yuki the bag as she grabbed it and said, "Thanks Daddy, you're so thoughtful." As Yuki ate her food Jackpot merged onto the I-5 freeway and headed back to San Diego.

9 HO'LLYWOOD

It had been 6 weeks, and Jackpot had stacked $25,000. He now had enough to make a few power moves and go on the road. First thing JP did was upgrade all of Yuki's wardrobe, and we're not talking about Fam-Mart discounts and knockoffs, but the real shit. He knew that if he wanted to be the best, then he had to set himself apart from the rest. Even his bitch.

Not only that, but he knew that the streets was watching, and them hoes watch even closer. So he wanted to knock the best bitches out there that money could afford. They would wanna see what they were choosing into, but more importantly, Jackpot learned early that, a happy hoe is a good hoe. So he kept Yuki happy and spoiled her at all times. He bought her shit from BeBe, Gucci, Louis purses, Baby Phat for the track, Donna Karen for the club. Channel, M.A.C cosmetics, mink coats from Sax, which he purchased 75% off because he bought it in the summer. Truth be told, Jackpot bought more shit for Yuki then he bought for himself. While other pimps was spending most of their money on new cars and jewelry for themselves, Jackpot was investing in his bitch first, and for that very reason, Jackpot's bitch made the most on the track, always came home happy, never questioned his pimpin or made mad moves every 3 days, leaving or running away like most hoes did.

Yeah, Jackpot had shit mapped out to a science. He felt like, before Yuki, he was doing without so what's a little longer without copping shit? He thought, *but when I do cop some shit and finally splurge on myself, I'm a go big like a mutha fucka!* That was Jackpot's way of thinking. They'd be in the mall shopping and Yuki would always say, "why don't you buy yourself something Daddy?" Or, "I like the way you look in that." And Jackpot would just tell her, "nah Babe, it ain't time for that right now. I'm straight. Right now it's all about you. I'll have my time."

Yuki really respected him for that. It made her feel like he wasn't just using her for what she could do for him. It made her feel appreciated. And truth be told, it made her wanna work harder and give him the world. To return the favor. To do for him like he's done for her.

Jackpot also knew that by handling his business this way, when he finally did make a big purchase for himself, no matter how much he might of spent, the bitch wouldn't get jealous or question him about it. She'd actually be happy he finally did something for himself. So with that thought in mind, Jackpot did without for the first 6 months of her hoe'n, minus the bare necessities. 6 weeks into these 6 months Jackpot set out to hit the road and go cross country. It was time to step it up to the next level, and he couldn't do that sitting in Daygo. Not only that but, stay in one place too long, and your bitch gets hotter than a firecracker. So after getting Yuki new clothes, he went to Enterprise rent-a-car, dropped $1,200, and rented a car for a month. That way he could push it to the limit without putting a lot of wear and tear on his 510.

He also didn't wanna draw too much negative attention by being too flashy. The California license plates was bad enough. Add rims and a beating ass system, and all police see is, "drug runner!" Especially in the mid 90's. So Jackpot rented a full size Grand Am and went back home to pack.

"Hey Babe I'm back, you finish packing?" Jackpot asked, as he opened the door to their hotel room. They had been staying in hotel rooms every since they got in the game. Jackpot's mission was to stack on the road, come back home and buy a nice house. "Yeah Daddy I'm just about done."

"Well drop your furs and extra clothes off at my moms house, they'll be safe there," Jackpot said to Yuki, as she placed the remainder of the things she was gonna take in the suitcase and locked it up. Jackpot moved Yuki out her friends house 2 days after she chosed up and hadn't looked back since. They stayed in the Marriot downtown in a semi luxury suite. The spot was laid out.

Even with her living in a hotel, it was a big step up from living with her homegirl in a small bedroom she had to share in East Daygo. But as nice as the hotel was, it was nothing like having your "own" shit. A place you didn't have to pay an arm and leg for by day, or week. Shit, for the price they were paying to stay at the Marriot, in that suite, they could have rented a mini mansion in Eastlake or Bonita. So Jackpot made it his business to get a house when they came back. After checking out the hotel and leaving Jackpot's moms house, they got on the freeway and headed north. First stop...Los Angeles Sunset Blvd.

------$$$$------

"Wake up Babygirl, we're here," Jackpot said to Yuki as they merged off the Thorton exit and arrived in Hollywood. Hollywood was nothing like Daygo. People were everywhere. Big fancy cars, bright lights, the nightlife was active. This place looked and smelled like money. Yuki was eager to get out and work. She knew by all the $100,000 cars she saw that she would have no problem making $1,000 or better here.

She couldn't wait, and Jackpot knew it too. Both of them didn't say a word but was thinking the same thing. They just played it cool and took it all in. Once Jackpot arrived on Sunset Blvd. he started looking for signs of bitches and hoe activities. It didn't take long to find it. Once he passed the Denny's, all he saw was wall to wall hoes. It was like nothing he had ever saw in his life. Bitches on the track revealing it all in a way you couldn't believe unless you'd seen it yourself. Not only that, but hoes was everywhere. At least a hundred or so easy. Jackpot had never seen so many hoes in the same place at one time in his life. As he passed the Denny's he saw nothing but pimps standing in front of the 7-11 to the left across from the Guitar Center. "Damn, this mutha fucka here look like pimp central," Jackpot quietly whispered to himself, as he banged a right after passing the guitar center on the next corner. This put them on a side street. So Jackpot parked the car and laced his bitch.

"Alright bitch, I know you see what I see and all I see is money. So tonight your quota is $1,000 nothing less. Where in the Mecca, Hollywood. Stay sharp like a Gensu or #2 pencil. I know you saw all them pimps on the corner, and you know it's their job to sweat you. Don't worry about all that.

"Just stay in pocket like a wallet and everything a be alright. If you have any problems out there hit me on the hip asap. You know the code. I'll be riding up and down the track all night. I know you saw all them Hoes out there so, if you catch one of them unhappy Snow White bitches out there, don't hesitate to bring her home like the seven dwarfs.

"We're about to elevate our situation like the top floor of the Empire State Building. You understand bitch?"

"Yes Daddy."

"Alright then, get out there and show these bitches what it's all about. We came to get loot like a pirate and possibly bring a new bitch home and redirect her guidance."

"I know daddy. Don't worry, I got you. I know what I need to do.."

"Alright, when you make your first $500 hit me up if I hadn't already broke you yet. Meet me at the Denny's."

"Okay Daddy."

"Alright bitch get ta work." Yuki pulled down the visor, checked her hair and make-up to make sure everything was still intact, got out and headed for the track. Sunset was different from any other track that Yuki had worked before. Bitches here was hoe'n right in the polices face, and as long as they wasn't vice, cops let em. Hoes was turning dates at red lights and done by the time the lights turned green.

Yuki couldn't believe the shit she was seeing, but she liked it. She knew she was gonna hit big. *Fuck a $1000, my goal is 2 or better*, Yuki thought to herself, after witnessing just how much hoes was getting it. The only bitch that wasn't gonna make money here was a lazy one and that was far from Yuki. As soon as Yuki hit the track, a trick in a brand new Porsche tried to pick her up.

"Hey handsome, you looking for a good time tonight? Yuki asked, slumped over in his passenger side window with her arms resting on the door.

"Yeah, actually I was looking for a nice young lady to party with," The trick responded, calm and relaxed. You could tell he'd done this before. It was definitely not his first time. Yuki opened up the car door and got inside. "Are you a cop?" Yuki asked.

"No, how about you?"

"Of course not, would a cop do this?" Yuki pulled the left side of her BeBe spaghetti strap shirt down and revealed her breast.

"No, I guess not," the trick answered with a lustful devilish grin.

"Now do me a favor to prove you're not a cop either?"

"What?"

"Touch my tits and show me your dick." Now any right minded trick would love to cop a free feel, but a cop or vice officer wouldn't, and Yuki knew this. After the trick did what Yuki asked, they negotiated prices, drove to a secluded place near by, and handled their business.

Back on the track

Jackpot drove up to the 7-11 where he saw all the pimps hanging and got out to pop pimpin with em. "Wuss up playa, wut it do?" Jackpot said as he got out the car to no one pimp in particular.

"Nothing much, just a whole lotta pimpin!" one pimp answered, as him and Jackpot shook hands and introduced themselves.

"Jackpot Tha Pimp outta San Diego."

"Good Game, outta wherever the road lead me."

"Right right," Jackpot answered with a slight smirk. "So what the track looking like pimp?" Jackpot asked, trying to get the full rundown of the stroll.

"Shit, what you see is what you get. This track is wide open. A hoe can work till the sun come up and the tourist come out. After that you have to take it in because the popo's a sweat your bitch, but until then, it's prime time hoe'n going on in this mutha fucka jack, ya dig?"

"Hell yeah, that's what pimpin talking bout," Jackpot answered, rubbing his hands together softly like he was trying to keep warm. Just at that moment Jackpot's pager went off. It was Yuki. The page said **304*500**. *Damn, already?* JP thought to himself. It had only been 20 minutes since he dropped Yuki off and she already made $500. She never made that much that fast.

Shit, tonight's gonna be a good night, JP thought to himself as he said his goodbyes to the other pimps and headed for the designated drop spot that he instructed Yuki to meet him at earlier. As Jackpot pulled into the Denny's parking lot, he saw Yuki walking towards the car. Jackpot pulled up along side and picked her up.

"Hey Daddy, it's money out here!" Yuki said eyes beaming looking happy as a mutha fucka.

"I told you bitch. You're in Hollywood. Home of the stars, and with you being a star yourself, you couldn't do nothing but shine.

"You got that right Daddy." She handed him a wad of cash.

"I thought you only made $500 Babygirl? this is six!"

"Yeah, I got another quick hundred for a blow job on my way here to meet you. You always taught me that a real hoe can make a trick cum in 60 seconds or less. So that's exactly what I did."

"That's right bitch, good work. We finna bubble like Bazooka Joe in this bitch in a real way. Stay down so we can come up," Jackpot said as he let a eager Yuki out the car to get back to work. Jackpot recounted his money as he sat in disbelief of how booming it was out there. "Shit, I should have brung my ass out dis mutha fucka a long time ago." Daygo was the Payless to Sunset's Foot Locker. This was the big leagues.

Jackpot left his car parked at Denny's and walked to the track. He spotted a bad ass snow bunny with long blond hair, green eyes, slim waist, with a cat shape face. She looked like she weighed no more than 120 pounds. Jackpot started poppin P's at her immediately. "Wuss up hoe, you got eyes you got action. Now get wit Jackpot Tha Pimp and experience some real satisfaction. You know bitch, I'm desperately seeking Susan for a choosen, so fuck wit JP Tha Pimp where you're always winning and never losing. Yeah bitch, I see you cracking a smile like a safe, so now all you gotta do is let your next move be your best move, choose up and we'll be straight." Just at that moment, the bitch stopped dead in her tracks, turned around to face Jackpot and said, "is that right? Okay then, so what happens next?"

Jackpot couldn't believe his ears. *Is this bitch really choosen up, just like that?* he thought to himself. In all actuality he was shocked, but never did he let it show. "You know wuss next. Pay a pimp, so we can make this official like a referee wit a whistle." The hoe pulled some money out her purse and said, "I have $600."

"That's cool, it's a start. Now go put 4 more on top a that, then come back and holla at me. What's your name?"

"Kathy, but they call me Green Eyes."

"Alright then Green Eyes, are you formally under any instructions?"

"Yes, I work for Payday but I'm not happy."

"Alright, well here's my pager number. Go get the rest of that money up so I can serve pimpin some news. I'll take that $600 as a down payment." The bitch agreed, gave Jackpot the $600 and went back to work to get the rest. Jackpot went back to his car feeling happier than a hoe at a trick convention. The pimp god was blessing him with everything he'd ask for. He knew that as long as he continued to play the game fair, there was nothing he couldn't accomplish.

------$$$------

A few hours had passed when Jackpot got a page from Yuki. The page said **304*1000**. It was about 3 a.m. Jackpot was rolling up and down the track keeping his presence known and popping at hoes. It was 3 a.m. but felt like 10 p.m. Sunset was active, with no clear sign of dying down anytime soon.

Jackpot drove into the Denny's parking lot where he saw Yuki immediately, already waiting. She got in the car and handed her folks a wad of cash. "That's a $1000 more Daddy," Yuki said, with a proud look on her face like a woman who had just accomplished the unthinkable for her man.

"Good job Babe, that's what the fuck I'm talking bout, and the nights still active. Stay down a couple more hours. We gonna take it in around five."

"Okay Daddy." Yuki jumped out the car and went back to work. No sooner than Yuki got out the car, Jackpot's pager went off. He didn't recognize the number so he went straight to the pay phone and called it back. "Hello, who's paging JP?"

"This is Green Eyes, I got your money Daddy."

"Alright that's wuss up, where you at?"

"On the track next to Carls Jr."

"Alright bitch, walk down to the Denny's and I'll meet you there." They hung up the phone and Jackpot went inside of Denny's to wait for Green Eyes. About 10 minutes later she walked inside and sat down in the booth where Jackpot was waiting.

"Wuss up Green Eyes, so you got that choosers fee up?"

"I wouldn't have paged you if I didn't."

"Don't get smart hoe," Jackpot said, in a playful but serious tone. "Well break yo self bitch and let's see what cha got. Green Eyes handed Jackpot a nice size bankroll. He grabbed the wad and counted it out. It came out to $550, and with the money she had already given him earlier, that brought her grand total to $1,150. "Alright bitch, good job. Now let's go call this nigga and serve him some news." Jackpot went back outside to use the pay phone. "What's the number bitch?"

"323-555-1881." Jackpot dialed the number and waited for an answer. "Hello, who's this? the voice on the other end answered, sounding curious as to who was calling.

"Wuss up playa? Dis Jackpot Tha Pimp, Daygo's finest. I got some good news for you, and some bad news for you, either way I got news."

"Yeah, wuss dat?"

"Well the good news is, pimpin just came up on a new hoe. The bad news is, she use ta be yours but now she ain't no mo."

"Ah, wut the fuck you talkin bout?"

"What I'm talkin bout is, I have a banana in a newspaper for you. The banana is because your bitch Green Eyes just got pealed. The newspaper is because I'm serving you news about it. So go ahead and break that plate because the bitch won't be making supper tonight pimpin."

"Ah man fuck dat hoe. She ain't nothing but a faggot anyway. I already pulled 2 benzes out the bitch, they don't call me Payday for nothing."

"Alright then pimp, I'll holla."

"Yeah whatever." As Jackpot was hanging up the phone, Yuki was walking down the track towards him.

Perfect timing, Jackpot thought to himself. He called Yuki over and introduced her to her new wife-in-law. "Yuki, this is your new wifey Kathy, also known as Green Eyes. Green Eyes, this is Yuki. Welcome to the family." The girls smiled and got acquainted. "How much you got on you?" Jackpot asked Yuki.

"I made $400 more daddy."

"Alright good job, excellent work. That brings your total to $2,000. Since the nights been so good to us all, we're gonna take it in early and get to know each other better." Jackpot had the best night of his life. Between the 2 hoes, he took in $3,150, bumped a new hoe, and was now "2 deep with no sleep." Life was good, and it was only gonna get better

10 TWO DEEP WITH NO $LEEP

"Rise and shine bitches!" Jackpot woke up his hoes.

"Good morning Daddy," Yuki said followed by Green Eyes still with cold in both their eyes. "What time is it? Yuki asked, rubbing her eyes, still trying to wake up.

"It's 3 p.m. I let ya'll sleep in, cause I knew we had gotten in late last night, or should I say this morning. I already paid the room for another night. Anyhow, ya'll bitches get in the shower and get dressed. We have a long day ahead of us, including getting you hoes some new clothes.

"Since we had such a good night last night, it's only right. Plus I gotta make sure you hoes is the best dressed bitches on the track tonight. You know ya'll representing this JP mackin, so let's get up and get it cracking." The bitches jumped up excited like 2 kids on christmas morning and hopped in the shower. While the hoes took their shower, "together" mind you, Jackpot re-counted his money. He put 2 G'z away in his stack and $1,150 in his pocket. *Yeah today is gonna be a good day, and a even better night.* 20 minutes later the hoes was out the shower, dressed, and ready to go.

After leaving the hotel, Jackpot took the bitches to Denny's for breakfast. Jackpot never really cared for Denny's because they served too much pork, and he didn't eat pork. But fuck that, when you can feed 2 bitches under $20 including tip, this was the way to go.

"2 grand slams and I'll have the steak and eggs," Jackpot told the waitress as they sat ordering their food. The waitress smiled, wrote down the order, picked up their menus and said, "coming right up."

While they waited for their food to arrive, Jackpot chopped it up with his bitches. 15 minutes later their orders had arrived. They ate up, left a tip, and headed out the door to start their day. Jackpot wasn't familiar with Hollywood. Since this was his first time in the city, he didn't have a clue as to where to go to get the bitches some fly clothes. But this was Hollywood, all you had to do was look out the window and pick a store. Shit was everywhere. This was a fact and realization Jackpot had figured out real fast.

One thing that tripped him out though, was the fact that Hollywood day and nights was complete opposites. Not only that but, Hollywood looked nothing like it did in the movies. In all actuality, Hollywood was ghetto. In the daytime, all the tourist came out to play, but the freaks came out at night. Hollywood resembled Time Square in New York after Disney took over. There was hustlers and weirdos everywhere. From human statues to con men hustling tourist with 3 card monte. Jackpot thought, *it's funny how the rich live right around the corner from the hood.* Shit, Bel-Air, Rodeo Drive, and the Hollywood Hills was only 15 minutes away from the madness. As Jackpot was having that thought, they passed by the Hollywood Chinese Theater. A few blocks up was the original Fredrick's of Hollywood. Good Game had told Jackpot about it last night when they were in front of the 7-11 chopping it up.

He told Jackpot that they had some fly ass hoe gear in there. All that banging shit that you see in the catalogues but never find in your local mall because their Fredrick's is usually limited to a few pieces.

Jackpot pulled into the parking lot, parked the car, and went inside.

"Hello may I help you?" said the clerk.

"No, not at the moment, but I'll definitely give you a holla if we need you," Jackpot said. The clerk smiled, said "okay," and went to assist a female customer who had just walked in.

"Alright bitches, go ahead and get something for tonight."

"Okay Daddy," both bitches answered in unison like a pair of backup singers for R.Kelly. As the hoes went off to look for an outfit, Jackpot looked around as well, taking mental note of all the merchandise Fredrick's had to offer for future reference. "Hey Daddy, how's this look?" Yuki asked, stepping out the dressing room in a semi see through cat suit, all black, clear bottom hoe shoes with a fake hundred dollar bill inside. The bitch looked bad as fuck in her skin tight outfit which fit her like a glove. "Damn Babe, you look like cat woman in that shit," JP said, jokingly smiling but visually aroused. "Yeah get that. I like it. Especially them hoe shoes with the money in em. Those shits is tight!" Yuki smiled, turned around, and walked back inside the dressing room to take off the outfit and put back on her regular clothes. Next, Green Eyes came out her dressing room looking equally as good, if not better, in a green lace top revealing one breast with a green flower shaped nipple cover that also brung out her eyes, a short ass mini skirt, ankle socks, and clear bottom shoes with gold trim.

The gold trim matched the sparkling gold embroidered dollar sign on her skirt. The bitch was looking like a million dollars.

"Damn bitch, now that's what I'm talkin bout. Don't change a thang. You're gonna kill em wit that outfit."

"Okay Daddy," Green Eyes responded, happy to have pleased her folks. After which, she walked back in the dressing room, took off the outfit, and handed it to the sales clerk.

"Will this be fine?" asked the clerk.

"Yes we'll take it," responded Green Eyes as she put her original clothes back on and walked out the dressing room. Shortly after, Yuki stepped out the dressing room with her clothes and took them to the front counter to ring them up.

"That ah be $328.00," the woman behind the register said as Jackpot pulled out his stack and payed for the clothes. "Thank you, come again," the woman said behind a fake smile as she handed the hoes the bags. "Alright you have a good one," JP said as they left the store, got in the car, and headed for the mall.

"Aye Green Eyes, where the mall at Babygirl?" Jackpot asked, knowing that a bitch that didn't know where the mall was located, was like a kid who didn't know how to find Toy "R" Us on his birthday.

"Turn right here Daddy at the next light."

"Alright bitches, I'd usually go and pick your outfits out for you, but seen and how ya'll had such a good night last night, I'm a peel ya'll both off some big faces and let ya'll do wut it do. Don't trip off of bringing me back change." Jackpot gave the bitches $500 each and let them out.

"Thanks Daddy," Yuki and Green Eyes both said grinning ear to ear like a circus clown at a birthday party.

Damn, I had to dip into my reserve stack for that, Jackpot thought to himself. He didn't really wanna spend that much. He wanted to stay within his $1,150 budget but the hoe clothes came out to be more than he expected. That was business though, and he knew he couldn't put those clothes back if he wanted to repeat last nights revenues. He also knew that with all the money them bitches made the night before, he had to give them at "least" $500 a piece to spend.

Shit, them hoes be counting even when they act like they're not, and a sure fire way to have a bitch start hiding money and stealing from her folks, is to not properly take care of the hoe after a good night. Good night being, after she done made a shit load of cash.

Jackpot also knew that he only had to do this in the beginning to keep the hoes hooked and happy, but after their closet is full to the brim with wall to wall shit, he could slow down and then take care of himself. Basically, take care of the hoes on the front end, so you can get rich and prosper on the back end. That way at the end of the day everyone is satisfied and happy. And Jackpot knows...a happy hooker, is a good hooker. So with that fact known, Jackpot dipped into his reserve stack in the glove compartment and handed them a couple more hundreds to make it $1,000.

"Alright bitches, page me when ya'll done. You know the code Yuki, let your wife-n-law know wuss up. I'll be close by, making my pimp rounds through the city."

"Okay Daddy," Yuki responded, as she kissed her folks on the cheek and got out the car. Green Eyes did the same, told her folks she'll see him soon and closed the door behind her as she got out as well.

Jackpot watched the happy hoes walk off arm-n-arm into the mall eager to get their shop on. Jackpot was making all the right moves, and because so, was coming up very fast within the game. Before driving off, he sat back and thought for a minute on how it was when he first got started and how far he came already in a short amount of time. But still in his heart he felt like this was just the beginning, and he had a long way to go to be where he really wanted to be in this game...which was the top! With that thought, he popped in his Too Short cassette, turned it up, and drove off.

While the hoes was in the mall shopping, Jackpot got himself familiar with Hollywood. He drove up and down the street. All up in through Sunset and back. Hollywood Blvd. to the Hollywood hills. Bel-Air to Rodeo, you name it he rode through it. *Shit, by the end of the day, I'll know this mutha fucka like the back of my hand,* Jackpot thought to himself. 3 hours later Jackpot's pager went off. *(304...304)* the code

Jackpot gave his bitches to use when they needed him. *Cool, these hoes is finally done shopping,* Jackpot thought to himself as he busted a u-turn by Tower Records on Sunset in route to go pick them up. When Jackpot arrived and pulled up to the mall, his bitches was already out front waiting for him.

"Hey Daddy," Yuki said, smiling as she opened the door.

"Can you pop the trunk please?" Green Eyes asked, equally smiling with 3 bags in her hands visibly from BeBe, Gap, and Nine West. Yuki's bags was from JC Penny's, Forever 21, and Wild Pair. You could tell both of the hoes was happier than a pig in shit. Jackpot hit the automatic trunk release button on the door panel and popped the trunk. The hoes put their bags inside, closed the trunk, and called it a day.

It was now 7:45 p.m. going on 8 and time to get ready for the nights endeavors. Jackpot went and got a hotel room 10 minutes away from the strip so that the hoes could get a little rest, freshen up, and go to work. The hotel was right on the side of T.G.I Fridays. So before going in he decided to let the hoes sit down and eat before going up and out to work. He knew it had been a long day and they probably hadn't gotten a chance to eat. He knew that when a bitch had her mind set on shopping, nothing else mattered. "Hey did ya'll eat anything at the mall?" Jackpot asked them both. "No Daddy, we was still full from brunch, but I am kinda hungry now." Yuki said, rubbing her stomach like a hungry convict in the penitentiary getting ready for chow.

"You too Green Eyes?" JP asked.

"Yeah I could use a little bite to eat." Green Eyes responded, looking equally as hungry.

"Alright then, we'll eat first, then go upstairs, get a little rest and head to work." Jackpot told em, as they walked over to Fridays, sat down, and got something to eat.

Back At The Hotel

"Alright bitches listen up." Jackpot spoke like a commander and chief getting ready for battle. "Tonight's our night. Last night was good but tonight's gonna be great. You hoes is looking like mutha fuckin stars out in this piece so there ain't no way ya'll not finna get money. Green Eyes, since this is the 1st time I'm setting you back down on the track since serving Payday news, it's a good chance he gon be on you tryna get you back, riding down on you hard. If he does, just keep it hoe'n head down in pocket like a wallet and keep it pushing."

"I know Daddy." Green Eyes said, nodding her head up and down like she know what's up. Jackpot continued. "Yuki, you already know how infatuated these tricks be with your fine asian ass. You're a rare breed out here like a Yorkie in the hood, so make these tricks pay as such. Between your green eyes, and your asian persuasion," Jackpot looked at them both. Ya'll shouldn't be excepting anything under $100. We playing fa big stakes out here. And the only way to hit it big is to play ta win." After Jackpot finished up his pep talk, the hoes was motivated and eager to get his money. "We got it Daddy, we know what to do. Tonight's gonna be good." Yuki said, confident ready to make her money. "Hell yeah, I'm ready ta get it!" Green Eyes said, right after fixing her outfit and putting a few condoms in her purse.

"Alright hoes, well nuff talking. Go out there, do what you do and make your Daddy proud. If ya'll have any problems, ya'll know the number. Anything over $500 hit me up and meet me at the drop spot to break yo' self."

"Okay Daddy." the hoes said, as they walked out the hotel room and headed for the track. Jackpot laid on the bed, put his hands behind his head and looked at the clock that was to his left on the dresser. *10:00 p.m. perfect timing,* Jackpot thought to himself, as he felt in his bones..."this, is gonna be a good night."

------$$$$------

"Bitch get the fuck up wit your lazy ass and get ready for work!" Payday said to his bottom hoe still visibly upset at the fact that he got knocked for and lost his hoe Green Eyes the night before. "Bitch you lazy. It's 10:00 and your ass is still in this mutha fucka! what you waiting for, an invitation? See that's all that fuckin weed you be smoking. You got 5 fuckin minutes to be outta here before I have 5 fuckin fingers across your face!" Payday's bitch jumped up with the quickness, got dressed, and was on the track in less than 4.

She knew not to force her folks hand when he was pissed, and she damn sure wasn't gonna be the scape goat or punching bag for him losing one of his bitches. Truth be told, Green Eyes was his top notch hoe. She out-shined his bottom every night. His bottom was a 30 year old vet name Shasha. She was black and passed her hoe prime. Shasha always saw Green Eyes as a threat and envied her. Though she was smart enough not to let it show around her folks. But truth be told, she was a pure hater and glad to see Green Eyes gone.

"Man fuck this shit! Who the fuck this bitch think she is? Nobody leaves Payday Tha Pimp. This hoe got me fucked up!" Payday said to himself out loud, pacing back and fourth in his room. The more he thought about Green Eyes being gone, the angrier he got. Who the fuck is Jackpot anyways? I never heard of this nigga. *Ain't no way some chili pimpin mutha fucka finna knock me for my bitch.* With that last thought in mind, Payday grabbed his car keys off the dresser, left the hotel room, and went to look for Green Eyes.

------$$$$------

"Fuck that mutha fucka. Don't get mad at me cause you slacking in your macking. Ain't my fault the bitch ran off," Shasha said to herself, walking the track mad at how her folks had came at her before she left. "Hey girl," a voice said from afar. Shasha looked across the street. It was a hoe name Katt that worked for a pimp name Fuk-A-Bitch out of East Oakland. "Hey girlfriend, Shasha said back, acknowledging her presence. Katt walked across the street to where Shasha was standing. "So girl, how long you been down?" Shasha asked. "Since 8, I made about $350 so far, but you know the night's still young."

"Yeah I just touched down so I haven't even broke luck yet."

"Yeah tonight's my last night in Hollywood. I think we're going to Frisco tomorrow. My Daddy said bitches is getting some good money out there."

"Really?"

"Yeah, you know out here it's too many white bitches to compete with."

"Yeah tell me about it. I barely made my quota last night."

"Bitch, get ta work and quit ho'cializing!" Payday screamed from his 500 big body Benz as he pulled up along side of the 2 bitches walking. "See, that's why you always having a hard time making your money, because you're doing more talking than sucking and more walking than fuckin. Now git yo ass ta work bitch and don't let me tell you again," Payday said, then looked Shasha in the eyes and said with all sincerity, "next time I catch you out here talking, it better be to a trick or bitch you're finna bring home. Now git bitch!"

As Payday drove off, Shasha rolled her eyes when she knew her folks was too far gone to see, sucked her teeth and went to work. "He fuckin make me sick! Alright girl let me get to work before dis nigga get ta trippin. I'll holla at you later."

"Alright girl, I know how it is. My folks be trippin too," Katt said as she too went back to work before her folks caught her ho'cializing and put down a similar demo on her the way Payday did to Shasha.

------$$$$------

"Wuss up pimp?" Fuk-A-Bitch said to Payday, standing in front of 7-11 as he pulled up in his ride and parked.

"Wut it do playa?" Payday said, getting out the car greeting his patna with a pimp shake and one arm hug.

"Shit, can't call it, the line always busy."

"Right right, no doubt," Payday said back. "So you knocked a new hoe huh? I saw Green Eyes with this asian bitch working earlier. That hoe was bad!"

"Hell nah pimp! I got knocked for that hoe last night. I'm actually looking for the bitch," Payday said, looking mad than a mutha fucka.

"Damn P, say it ain't so. Green Eyes was a bad little hoe too. Oh well, ex-bitch to the next bitch. It happens to the best of us. We know the game, cop-n-blow, touch-n-go. You never know what's on these bitches minds. That's why all we can do is get it one day at a time." Payday knew that he was right, but at the same time, he wasn't tryna hear that. "Yeah well, when I catch the bitch out here, I'm on her like an asian on rice. You can best believe, pimpin gon be on that hoes heels."

"I feel you pimp, cause the bitch could've just made a mad move in such." Payday nodded his head in agreement and said..."Exactly, you know how these bitches do. Always think the grass is greener on the other side until another pimp get in that ass 10 times worst. Then the bitch wanna come back home."

"Shit, you ain't never lied. Katt left and came back like 4 times. When the last nigga put a pimp stick to her ass and made her stand in the corner with one foot up like a flamingo, that put an end to all that running away shit," Fuk-A-Bitch said, as they both laughed.

(304*625) the pager read as it went off followed by, *(304*911)*. This was the first time the emergency code was used so Jackpot knew it was a problem

and had to be something serious. Jackpot jumped up with the quickness, grabbed his car keys off the nightstand and headed for the streets. *Shit, I wonder what's wrong. Police, vice, did my bitch get robbed or kidnapped? Please don't say she got raped,* Jackpot couldn't help but think to himself as he drove down the track.

304*911... 304*911. Shit! wuss going on? Now I know it's serious. Jackpot's pager kept going off. 2 minutes later he was by the Denny's where he saw Yuki looking calm and waiting in the parking lot. Jackpot pulled up, jumped out and asked, "Wuss wrong?"

"Nothing Daddy, I just paged you because I had $625 on me."

"Then why did you put 911?"

"I didn't." Said Yuki. "**Shit!** That must've been Green Eyes then," Jackpot said under his breath but still loud enough where Yuki could hear him.

"Wuss wrong Daddy?"

"I don't know yet. You seen your wifey?" Jackpot asked looking worried as a virgin boy in a catholic church with a pedophile priest.

"No, not since earlier when we first came out. She turned a date, then I got one and been busy ever since."

"Alright Yuki, go back to work. I gotta go check some shit out."

"Alright Daddy, is everything okay?"

"Bitch, just do as I said. I'll talk to you later." As Yuki went back to work, Jackpot went back on the track to look for Green Eyes. *Damn I'm slipping. Why didn't I buy Green Eyes her own pager?* Jackpot drove up and down the track, with no clear sign of his bitch in sight.

------$$$$------

"Bitch, you think you can just leave me like some sucker ass nigga? I made you hoe. I brung you in the game, and I'll take your faggot ass out," Payday said to Green Eyes, as he had her hemmed up in a back alley off the track where no one could see.

"Bitch you was nothing but a pretty face when I met you, standing at a bus stop with no money and no place to go. Now that I taught you how to hoe and get doe you gon run off and pay some other mutha fucka?" Payday was hot and Green Eyes was scared to death. She didn't say a word. She knew what Payday was capable of, especially when he got mad. She saw him beat the shit out of Shasha a few times, for something as simple as being $20.00 short of her quota, but he had never put hands on her. This was one of the reasons why Shasha envied her so much. This was also the reason why Green Eyes wanted to get away from him, because she knew that it would only be a matter of time before Payday was beating on her as well. "Oh now you ain't got nuthin ta say huh bitch, What, trick got cha tongue?"

"No Daddy...it's just..."

"Oh now I'm Daddy again huh? Bitch get your mutha fuckin ass in the car before I knock your fuckin teeth out! You really got this pimpin fucked up hoe." Payday led the bitch by the neck, opened the car door, and pushed her inside. As he walked around to the drivers side to get in, Green Eyes knew that this was probably gonna be her only chance to escape. If she didn't, who knows what would be her fate. Just as Payday opened his door and got half way inside the car, Green Eyes rushed open her side door, got out the car, and ran for dear life, like a bat out of hell.

------$$$$------

As Jackpot was driving down the track, he spotted Green Eyes looking frantic, visibly shook up, running out of a dark alley. Jackpot quickly pulled over to come to her rescue and assess the situation.

"Daddy help!...help!...he's gonna kill me!" Green Eyes said to Jackpot as she rushed to open the door and get in the car.

"Wuss wrong babygirl, who's gonna kill you?" Jackpot asked, looking concerned and equally worried. Just as he spoke, his question was answered in the form of Payday running out of the alley, fist balled up, looking like a mad man ready to kill someone. Jackpot quickly got out of the car to confront the man he saw approaching, who at the time, had no idea was Payday.

"Yo wuss hatn'n here, we got a problem?" Jackpot said with his arms out looking like Jesus on a cross.

"Hell yeah we got a problem. That's my bitch you got in the car and you need to mind your business square!" Payday said, also not realizing that he was talking to Jackpot the pimp.

"Whoa whoa, slow your roll to a snails pace. 1st of all, ain't nothing square about me but my money after I fold it. 2nd, that there bitch right there, is my hoe. I don't know who you is or what you heard, but let me be the first to inform you that she's up under my instructions. She's representing this JP Mackin in a real hoe fashion."

When Jackpot finished talking, and Payday realized who he was face to face with and talking to, he blew up.

"Nigga I don't give a fuck about your pimpin mane, dis Compton Crip. Nigga if you wanna bang we can bang!"

"Whoa whoa playa, I thought we was promoting pimpin not gang banging."

"Nigga I told you, I don't give a fuck about all that fly shit you talking. Save that shit for them bitches. This is not the 70's nigga, I'm a gangsta, and like I said, that's my bitch nigga!"

"Well I'm sorry to hear that Mr Gangsta because unlike you, I'm a pimp, and I respect the game as such. Now whether it's 1970 or 2010 your bitch chose me and that's just what it is. Now I tried ta handle this like a couple of gentlemen but don't get it fucked up, you ain't dealing wit a punk, and we can definitely get into some gangsta shit. So wut choo wanna do Mr Compton?" Jackpot said serious as all outdoors looking Payday dead in his eyes.

"Fuck you cuzz," Payday responded.

"Nah don't fuck me, fuck the bitch," Jackpot said, still with no visual signs or intentions of backing down.

"Oh you tough now huh?" Payday said with a wicked sly smirk on his face rubbing his hands together and biting his bottom lip.

"Nah I ain't tough, you're the tough guy. I'm just your friendly neighborhood pimp tryna keep it pimpin wit cha. But I will say my patience is starting to run a little thin. Not only that playa, but you're ready to kill and spill blood over a bitch that don't even wanna be with you. Now that shit makes about as much sense as a three dollar bill pimp. If the bitch wanna go, let her go. You sit her down, all she gonna do is run off the first chance she get anyways, or even worst, get the cops involved outta fear. Now I know you're not tryna catch a case behind the hoe." Jackpot could sense and see that he was finally starting to get through to Payday because he started to calm down a bit, put his hands down by his sides and talk sensibly.

"Yeah alright, take the bitch. I'll see you around," Payday said, as he backed up slowly towards his car, got inside, and took off. "Man I think this sucka for love ass nigga's gonna be a problem." Jackpot said to himself. At that moment Jackpot knew it was time to get back on the freeway to their next destination and keep it pushing. Trust taught Jackpot that an ounce of prevention, is better than a pound of cure. And he knew that Payday was far from over with sweating his bitch. "You okay?"

"Yeah Daddy, I'm alright. Just a little shook up."

"It's alright babygirl I'm here now. You won't have to worry about that lame ass nigga fuckin with you anymore. Tonight we're hitting the road and leaving for San Francisco. We're gonna see what Fillmore has to offer." Just at that moment Jackpot's pager went off. (*304*700*). "Right on time," Jackpot said to himself. It was Yuki, and perfect timing too, because Jackpot was ready to shake Hollywood like some Vegas dice, before things got any worse.

"Did you make anything before that nigga pushed up on you?" Jackpot asked Green Eyes already assuming that the answer was no. "Yeah Daddy, he didn't get me for my money. He tried, but I always keep my money in my pussy, so he couldn't find it."

"Alright, that's wuss up. How much you make?" Jackpot asked, proud as well as impressed of how smart and sharp his bitch was for hiding her money in her love box.

"Only $600, but that was just 2 dates. I was about to page you to come get it and then that's when I saw Payday approaching me, so I put in 911 instead of 600."

"That's cool babygirl. Let's go pick your wifey up and blow this mutha fucka."

------$$$$------

Oh here comes daddy now, Yuki thought to herself as she saw her folks car approaching from a distance. Jackpot pulled into the Denny's parking lot, rolled down his window, and instructed Yuki to get in. "Hey Daddy, what's wrong?" Yuki asked, visibly noticing that something was wrong by the expression on her folks face.

"Nothing I'm tryna get into right now. It's just time to shake the spot and keep it moving," Jackpot said with a serious enough tone that Yuki knew best to leave well enough alone rather than question and ask why. *Damn, I was making money out here too,* Yuki couldn't help but think to herself.

Well, at least I made the money back I spent on these hoes earlier, JP thought to himself as he broke Yuki and counted his money. "Alright bitches, we finna call it a night. 1st we're gonna get some grub, head back to the hotel, pack, and relax. Come checkout time, we're outta here and headed for Frisco," Jackpot said, as he put the car in drive and drove off.

11 $AN FRANCI$CO

"Wake up bitches, we're here," Jackpot said as they crossed over the golden gate bridge.

"Is that Alcatraz?" Yuki asked, pointing to the legendary, old famous run down prison that once held Alcapone.

"Yep, sure is Babygirl." Jackpot responded.

"You think before we leave we can take a tour Daddy?" Green Eyes asked, equally excited about the prison.

"Sure, I don't see why not. As long as you bitches make ya'll money, we can do whatever ya'll like," Jackpot responded, gripping the steering wheel with one hand leaning to the side. "Alright bitches, it's been a long ride, so we're gonna go get something to eat, stretch our feet, and check into a hotel."

"Okay Daddy." Both Yuki and Green Eyes responded in unison like 2 eager kids on their way to Disneyland. As always, Jackpot looked for a hotel and place to eat. "I feel like a nice pizza, how bout ya'll?"

"That sounds good."

"Yeah it's been a while since I had pizza," Green Eyes and Yuki responded.

"Alright, then we'll kill 2 birds with 1 stone. First we'll get the hotel room, go upstairs, look in the yellow pages and order a pizza. That way, we can eat and relax at the same time."

"Cool."

"Alright, the girls responded. Yuki followed by Green Eyes, as Jackpot turned onto Fillmore St. in the Fillmore district, and got a room at a one star hotel not too far from the track. Jackpot ordered a large pizza and a 2 litter of sprite with buffalo wings. The hoes took a shower and freshened up while they waited for the food to arrive. 30 minutes later, 2 finished showers, and a knock on the door..."**Pizza!**" A voice from the hallway said. Jackpot opened the door to find a teenage boy no more than 17 standing before him with a large pizza and brown paper bag.

Jackpot handed the delivery boy $30 and told him to keep the change. After which, he closed the door. Jackpot and the hoes ate the pizza and got some rest. That way, everyone would be game woke, fresh, an at their best tonight, including Jackpot.

By ten o' clock that evening, everyone was up, dressed, and ready to hit the track like an olympic sprint runner in Barcelona. While the hoes was on the track, Jackpot was doing as he always did in a new city, getting to know the streets. He drove all through the slums and made a mental note of everything. What streets looked safe, which ones didn't. What type of stores and restaurants was in the area, etc, etc, etc. After driving around for about 45 minutes, he parked the car off of Fillmore St. and got out to stretch his legs. This is when he noticed a clean all white cadillac approaching. The car pulled into a gas station across the street from where Jackpot was standing. When the man stepped out of the vehicle, you could visibly tell that he was pimpin.

He had on a slick italian suit, matching fedora and gators. What really set it off and put him out there was the three white bitches that stepped out the back. Jackpot couldn't believe his eyes. Not because of the pimp or the fact that he got out of a smooth looking caddie with 3 of the baddest bitches he ever saw, but more or so because the pimp looked to be about 60, and his hoes...not a day over 18. Jackpot thought, *now this is how a pimp should look in his prime.* This cat had his shit tighter than most of the younger pimps Jackpot had ran into, befriended, and got to know. Though Jackpot didn't know it at the time, he was actually in the presence of a legend.

The man across the street was Fillmore Slim, one of the coldest macks to ever live. He was from the old school and had real old school game. Back when pimps wore platforms, bell bottoms, and multi colored minks. Now it was the mid 90's and he was still doing it big. He had 2 stables of hoes. Guess you could call them 1st string and 2nd string, because if you saw them all in one place at the same time together, you'd thought you was looking at an all girl football team or some shit. He had over 10 bitches, all hoes, all different flavors. From vanilla to chocolate, and everything else in between. While Fillmore Slim was inside the gas station, one of his hoes was outside pumping his gas into the caddie. Jackpot observed the entire scene like a director in a movie and took it all in. This just motivated Jackpot and made him wanna step it up further. Fillmore Slim came out the gas station convenient store as his hoe was finishing up pumping gas. The 4 got back in the caddie, started the car, and drove off into the moon lit night.

------$$$$------

"Alright bitches I ain't fuckin around tonight. I expect you hoes to make ya'll quota tonight, no excuses. I don't give a fuck if it take ya all night and day, 14 hours flat you don't come in without my scratch," Fuk-A-Bitch said to his hoes as he set them down to work.

"Katt, you keep an eye on that new bitch," he whispered in her ear, about a hoe he knocked in Hollywood the night before as she got out the car.

"Okay Daddy." Katt responded, as she closed the door and went to work. Fuk-A-Bitch had 3 hoes. All of them black. They hit the track looking like 3 sophisticated hood rats.

Fuk-A-Bitch went into his left inside pocket and pulled out a swisher sweets cigarillos, filled it with purp, and lit it up as he watched his bitches work. F.A.B (Fuk-A-Bitch) wasn't into babysitting his hoes, but since he had a new bitch that wasn't even 24 hours old, he figured he'd keep an eye on her and his stable while they worked for the first 1/2 hour or so. Or until his blunt was done. As F.A.B took in the mind altering fumes of the purp into his lungs and blew out a thick cloud of smoke, he spotted a familiar face. *Oh shit, is dat that hoe Green Eyes?* F.A.B thought to himself as he took in another look while adjusting his eyes to see her better. "Yep, that is that bitch," answering his own question, as Green Eyes became a lot clearer standing under a street light on the corner not too far away from where F.A.B was parked and sitting. F.A.B continued to watch the bitch as he finished smoking his blunt. He watched her pull date after date, at least 3 in the short amount of time it took him to finish the slim blunt he was smoking. After he was done, he started the car and drove to the nearest pay phone.

------$$$$------

Ring...Ring!!!

"Hello," Payday answered.
"Wuss up pimp? dis Fuk-A-Bitch."
"Hey wuss up F.A.B, wuss crackin playa?"
"Shittt, a whole lotta pimpin!"
"Right right, so what do I owe the pleasure? you only call when it's important or something serious on your mind."
"Man, serious as a heart attack pimp. Guess who I just saw up here in Frisco on Tenderloin?"
"Who?" Payday asked, curious as a insecure wife with her husbands pager on the dresser.
"That bitch Green Eyes. Yep, I just saw the bitch pull a few dates while I was watching my stable. The hoe's getting it too. Bitch in and outta cars quicker than you can say shit."

"Get the fuck outta here, is that right? That old sucka ass nigga musta took her up there last night or this morning, cuzz, I haven't seen the bitch since yesterday, and I damn sho was looking foe her. Okay that explains a lot. Good looking out pimp, I'll be down that way tomorrow."

"Alright."

"Peace."

"One." They hung up the phone and ended the conversation.

*(304*75*500)* Jackpot's pager went off. 75 was Green Eye's code symbolizing (G-E) for the 7th and 5th letter in the alphabet. After the incident that took place the night before, Jackpot wasn't taking anymore chances. So first chance he got, on their way to San Francisco, Jackpot bought Green Eyes her own pager and gave it to her.

Jackpot drove down the track on Tenderloin looking for Green Eyes. He spotted her 2 minutes later standing at a bus stop looking like she was waiting for the express. That was the game that most seasoned hoes knew to do to keep the vice off their ass and from asking questions.

Jackpot pulled up along side her, rolled down the passenger side window and told her to break herself. Green Eyes reached into her bra and took out a wad of cash equaling $500 and handed it to him. "Good job bitch, so far so good. Stay down so we can come up," Jackpot instructed Green Eyes, as she nodded, said okay and went back to work.

Later on that night, back at the hotel

"Tonight was another good night bitches. Between the 2 of you, we brung in $2,200. Not as good as Hollywood but shit, this ain't Hollywood so I ain't mad at you." Jackpot spoke while tallying up the nights earnings, as both his bitches sat across the hotel bed looking prouder than a student's parents at graduation.

Jackpot continued to speak giving his nightly pep talk that he always gave to his hoes before and after work. He told them both, job well done and to get in the shower. While the hoes took their shower, Jackpot pulled out a sack of purple haze that he copped earlier while the hoes were out working, a box of cigarillos, and rolled a fat blunt, after gutting the cigar of it's tobacco filled contents. Jackpot then put the blunt into the ashtray that was sitting on top of the night stand, laid across the queen size bed, and waited for his bitches to get out the shower, as he grabbed the remote to the television, turned it on, and flipped through the channels.

When Yuki and Green Eyes got done with their shower, they both got in the bed with Jackpot on either side buck necked.

"Pass that blunt Babygirl," Jackpot said to Yuki while pointing at the purp filled blunt on the night stand. Yuki was surprised to see the blunt, due in fact that she never saw Jackpot smoke or do drugs. Shit, he barely drank. And if he did, it was never beer or heavy liquor but more like champagne or exotic wine.

"Tonight we're gonna relax and celebrate to all the hard work ya'll been putting in. As well as the boat load of cash ya'll been making and bringing home to Daddy every night." Jackpot fired up the blunt. Jackpot took a big hit followed by a short one, held in the haze for a second and blew it out. He then passed the blunt to Yuki who had never smoked weed before. This was her first time and you could tell right away by how she held the blunt with her thumb and index finger way at the back like it was already a doobie. You could also tell by the way she took a small baby hit, and blew the smoke out right away without holding it in long enough to really take effect. Still being, this was chronic. Not some of that backyard boogie bullshit mutha fucka's be smoking for $60 an ounce. So even with the baby hits, and this being her first time, Yuki was about to be higher than a mutha fucka.

After Yuki finished with her hit, she passed the blunt to her wifey Green Eyes who knew how to hit the weed all too well. Unlike Yuki, this wasn't her first time smoking, and you knew it right away by how she took a long pull, held it in, and blew it out her nose.

"Show off," Yuki playfully said to herself but just loud enough for everyone to hear as she watched her wife-n-law hit the blunt and pass it to her folks. Half way through the blunt, the haze began to take effect on the trio as they sat back relaxed, senses tuned in and acute.

Yuki began to feel a tingle throughout her body as she took her final hit of the blunt. The purp had her feeling horny as she felt her pussy tingle and start to get wet. Green Eyes was feeling the effects as well. Jackpot noticed, as he took his final pull of the blunt, put the doobie out in the ashtray and got ready for what was sure to come next. A long night of passionate 3 way fucking.

Jackpot took off his clothes and got undressed, then laid back down on his back with his bitches equally laying above each arm with his hands around their waist. Both bitches moved in closer to lay on his chest. Each head took up one peck. The bitches faces was so close they could've been mistaken for siamese twins joined at the head.

Jackpot began seductively running his fingers through Yuki and Green Eyes long beautiful hair as the 2 girls started to kiss. Yuki caressed the side of Green Eyes cheek with her right hand, ever so gently, like a newborn baby not even a week old fresh home from the hospital. Green Eyes slowly grabbed the back of Yuki's head with her left hand and brung her in closer, as she delicately placed her tongue into Yuki's mouth and kissed her deep. The site of Jackpot watching his 2 hoes go at it like 2 lesbian porn stars in San Fernando Valley made his dick hard.

As his soldier stood strong, erect, and at a stand still, Yuki grabbed his dick while still kissing her wifey and began to stroke it slowly. While Yuki stroked his dick, Green Eyes played with his balls. She was extra careful and gentle as only a pro knows how to be. Jackpot then grabbed a hand full of hair and pulled them apart, then lowered his head and 3 way kissed them both.

Tongue, lips, and saliva all joined as one. As the sweet scent aroma from the hoes wet, obviously turned on pussies began to fill the room, Jackpot continued to kiss Green Eyes, controlling her head like a joystick, still with a hand full of hair in his tight grip, as he used his other hand to slowly push and guide Yuki's head down towards his erect and throbbing penis. On her way down she softly kissed his chest, stomach, and mid section, before grabbing his 9 and a 1/2 inch manhood and placing it in her mouth. The sensation of Yuki's warm tongue and purple haze filled high sent chills through Jackpots body and caused him to curl his toes. He quickly regain composure, so as to not show any type of weakness and keep it pimpin. Jackpot grabbed a handful of Green Eye's breast with his left hand and took it into his mouth, as she closed her eyes, let out a slight moan, and put her head back. Jackpot sucked, nibbled, and gently pulled on her pink nipple, working his tongue like a hungry snake.

Yuki teased and licked the shaft of Jackpot's dick like a cold popsicle on a summers day, as he played with her pussy, all the while feeling her sweet nectar. Wet and dripping from excitement. Green Eyes palmed the back of Yuki's head while she bobbed up and down on Jackpot's dick. Then Jackpot took Green Eye's titties out of his mouth and guided her down south as well to join her wifey.

Yuki took Jackpot's dick out of her mouth, still holding it in her right hand and watched Green Eyes suck it. As Jackpot watched his 2 hoes tag team his dick like a WCW wrestler, he continued to play with both of their pussies as he felt their clits grow twice in size.

Green Eyes took all 9 and a 1/2 inches into her mouth, down to the balls. Giving a whole new meaning to the phrase..."deep throat." Green Eyes and Yuki then began sucking Jackpot'sdick together, meeting at the head where their tongues became 1. The veins in Jackpot's dick looked like they wanted to explode. As the bitches began to kiss, Jackpot got up and watched his hoes go at it. Yuki sucked on Green Eyes breast while Green Eyes played and sucked on hers. Green Eyes laid Yuki down on her back and started sucking on her pussy. Yuki grabbed and clenched the sheets as Green Eyes made small circles around her clit. Yuki arched her back as her body began to tremble and feel numb as a drunk passed out with a bottle of whiskey.

Green Eyes spread Yuki's lips apart and hummed on her clit as Yuki climaxed to elevation and screamed a passionate cry of satisfaction. Yuki then turned Green Eyes over and returned the favor. Yuki climbed over Green Eyes in a 69 like a Pisces.

Jackpot eased around Yuki and placed his dick inside her pussy. Yuki moaned as she continued to eat and lick Green Eye's pussy like a now-or-later. Jackpot started fucking Yuki harder. Teasing her with the tip of his dick while she begged for him to fuck her harder.

"Fuck me Daddy, fuck me. Fuck this pussy!" Green Eyes got up from under Yuki and sat side by side, with her in the doggy style position, playing with Yuki's titties and tongue kissing her in the mouth as Jackpot continued to fuck her. Jackpot pulled his dick out and placed it inside of Green Eyes. Her pussy was tight and wet. When he pulled back, her pussy would pull him back inside like a suction cup. Every time he pulled back, he could see the pink inner lining of her pussy holding on for dear life. Gripping his dick like elastic. Green Eyes fucked him back by pushing into him and making her butt roll like a stripper in a titty bar. Jackpot could feel her pussy muscles tighten up on him with each stroke. At that moment Green Eyes tensed up, put her face in the pillow, and bit the covers to keep from screaming.

"Uh uh, I'm cum'n Daddy!" Green Eyes said, as she came and squirted like a water pistol. When she came, it took Jackpot by surprise, because he never had a bitch squirt before.

"Damn bitch, so you're a squirter huh?" Jackpot said, turned on by the fact. Feeling her warm flow as he pulled out and watched the cum run out her pussy. Yuki sucked Green Eyes cum and pussy juice off Jackpot's dick as Green Eyes laid face down, twitching with aftershocks from the big orgasm she just had. Yuki began to suck Jackpot's dick harder and faster, while stroking it with her hands at the same time. Jackpot grabbed her head with both hands and fucked her mouth. Yuki could feel Jackpot's dick swelling up as he busted a fat load and came. Yuki swallowed like it was breakfast milk, without missing a beat or spilling a drop until Jackpot's dick got sensitive and couldn't take it anymore. After the hour and a half freak session was over, they fell into a deep coma like sleep, and called it a night.

Knock...knock...knock!!!

"Room service!" Everyone was awakened by the knock on the door and house keeper stating that it was check out time. Jackpot looked at the clock on the nightstand, now realizing that they had slept through the morning, he got up, put his boxers on, and went to the door to let the housekeeper know that they would be staying another night. The housekeeper asked if he needed anymore wash cloths and towels. Jackpot said, "yes thank you," as she handed him a fresh bunch and went on her way. By this time, Jackpot's hoes was up with that morning after sex glow that most bitches have after being fucked good the night before. Jackpot sat on the edge of the bed and rolled a blunt while his hoes jumped in the shower and got ready to start their day. While the hoes got ready, doing their make-up and fixing their hair, Jackpot smoked a blunt and counted his money.

"Since we getting off to a late start today, we won't have enough time to site see, but I will get ya'll some new shit to wear tonight," Jackpot said, taking $600 out of his stack and placing it to the side. The hoes said thank you and finished getting dressed. Jackpot rolled another blunt, finishing up the 2 dubs of purp he had bought and told the hoes, "this one's for ya'll," as he got in the shower and washed up.

As Jackpot showered, the hoes fired up the blunt, turned the T.V. on to B.E.T, relaxed and zoned out watching videos on Rap City. Jackpot got out the shower and put on his Karl Kani jeans and matching shirt, Gucci sneakers and Versace sunglasses. When the hoes saw Jackpot in his new outfit, their jaws hit the floor. Unbeknownst to them, Jackpot had bought this outfit in Hollywood while his hoes was shopping and he was touring the town. He ran into this hustler that was selling clothes and jewelry from his trunk, still with the price tags on them and everything. When the hustler told Jackpot he'd give him the entire fit for $300 he couldn't resist. Shit, the Versace frames cost that alone.

"Damn Daddy you look good." Green Eyes said with a serious and lustful look on her face.

"Don't he? And those glasses make you look extra sexy. I like the way you look in those." Yuki agreed and commented as well.

"Thanks Bitches. Well let's get out of here and get you hoes some gear, so ya'll can kill em on the track as always." The hoes jumped up quick-n-fast like a fire drill in middle school and ran out the door, eager to go shopping and get some new clothes. Jackpot went to the front desk of the hotel to pay for another night and asked the hotel manager where he could find the local mall or shopping center. The manager ran up another night and wrote down directions on how to get to the mall. Jackpot thanked the clerk, handed him a tip and left the office.

------$$$$------

"Alright hoes ya'll know the deal, same as always. Today we only getting one outfit because we gotta get this loot up. So here's $300 a piece. That's $100 for a top, $100 for a bottom, and $100 for some shoes, so ya'll should be more than straight. Page me when ya'll done. I'll be looking around and window shopping myself."

The hoes said okay to assure they understood. Jackpot handed them both $300. No sooner than that, the hoes were no where to be seen. Jackpot just laughed to himself and shook his head, like a father watching his kids run to the toy store eager to spend their allowance.

While the hoes shopped, Jackpot did as he said he was and window shopped. Making mental note of all the latest shit that he was gonna cop once his money was right. As far as he was concerned, he was back on his stack program which meant, anything less than $10,000 in his stack couldn't be touched or spent, at least not by him. He stood strong on that concept. That was his unwritten rule. Trust taught Jackpot that, you had to stack thousands before you could spend hundreds. He also told him to get that lawyer and bail bondsman money up first before making any major purchases because, you never know when it's gonna rain and storm in on your sunny day. So far, Jackpot's been lucky not to have had his bitches get picked up, go to jail, or catch a case. But in this line of work, Jackpot knew that going to jail was inevitable, and was only a matter of time. 2 hours had passed when Jackpot saw Yuki approaching him as he sat in the food court munching on a #4 from Burger King. "Hey Daddy."

"Hey Babygirl, you finished shopping?"

"Yeah."

"Where's your wifey at?"

"I saw her in Banana Republic, she said she'll be out soon. I told her to meet me at the food court when she's done."

"Alright, that's cool. You hungry?"

"Yes Daddy."

"You have any change left over?" Jackpot asked, knowing the answer was no.

"No, I barely had enough money to get my outfit Daddy."

"Um hum, I bet."

"Fa'real, I'm serious," Yuki said, in a playful wining, childlike voice. Jackpot just smiled and said, "it's cool, that's what I gave you the money for. Here's $10, go get yourself something to eat." Yuki thanked her folks, kissed him on the cheek, and went over to the chinese buffet to get some food. Shortly after, Green Eyes appeared from afar. Jackpot watched her as she approached and sat down. "Sup Babe, everything cool?"

"Yeah, I got something cute."

"Any change?"

"A little, like $6."

"Oh, really?" Jackpot said sarcastically 1 eyebrow raised with a smirk. Green Eyes playfully smacked him on the arm, sucked her teeth and smiled. "Well here, put this $5 with that and go get yourself something to eat." Green Eyes took the money, thanked her Daddy, and went to get some food. Jackpot checked the time on his pager. It was a little after 4.

Still making good time, he thought to himself, as he finished up his burger and took down his last 2 french fries. Green Eyes and Yuki sat down and ate their food while Jackpot sat on the other side of the table posted up, waiting for his hoes to finish so they could get back to the hotel, rest up a bit, and go to work. He wanted them to get an early start tonight, see and how as this wasn't Hollywood and the hoes was making less. Not only that, but the track out here started pumping the minute the sun went down. So Jackpot thought, *come seven o' clock, these bitches is getting active.*

------$$$$------

"Wuss up pimp? I'm here at the motel 6. I just arrived about an hour ago," Payday said speaking into the phone at the hotel. He had just checked in not even 5 minutes and was already calling F.A.B to get an update on Green Eyes, Jackpot, and their whereabouts. F.A.B informed Payday that he had secretly followed Green Eyes back to the hotel she was staying at last night after she had gotten off work. "Is that ritghttt? Hold up F.A.B, let me get a pen." Payday picked up the complimentary hotel pen off the dresser and note pad that came with the room and began to write. F.A.B gave Payday the address to the hotel he witnessed Green Eyes go into and believed she was staying at. "Good looking out pimp," Payday said as he jotted down the room number, tore the paper off the pad, and hung up the phone.

"Well well well," Payday said to himself, as he tightened his bottom and top lips across his teeth and let out a evil and sinister grin that would give the devil himself the chills. Payday grabbed his 16 shot nine which he nicknamed, "Nina Ross" from under the mattress, put the heater in his waist, safety on, pointing at his nuts. He grabbed the car keys off the night stand, opened and closed the door behind himself, got in his benz, started it up and took off.

------$$$$------

"How much you tryna spend?"
"$100."
"Oh for that we can definitely work something out." Green Eyes negotiated with the overweight, balding, mid 40's, white trick that stood before her, eager to sleep with the green eyed vixen with nothing but lust in his eyes. "I would like you to give me head."

"Not a problem sugar." Green Eyes opened the car door and got inside. "Turn up here at this next light sugar," Green Eyes said, in her most sensual and seductive voice. She could see the tricks little dick get hard just from the sound of her voice. Green Eyes instructed the trick to pull into a dark alley on a side street off the track. "Okay Honey first you have to pay, then you can play." Green Eyes said, licking the top of her lip with her tongue.

The trick reached into his pants pocket, pulled out his wallet, grabbed $100 and paid her. Green Eyes slid the $100 in her cleavage and pulled out a condom, all in one motion with the same hand. She could see a small lump in the tricks pants where his penis should be.

Green Eyes unzipped his pants and pulled them down enough to discover and reveal his boy size 5 inch penis sticking up like a small finger. "Oh it's so big." Green Eyes said in a seductive voice, obviously lying as the gullible trick smiled like she wasn't. Green Eyes opened the Trojan extra small condom with her mouth as she ripped open the package with her teeth, took out the rubber and placed it on his dick. As she rolled it down she noticed that it was only half way and already covering his whole penis.

Green Eyes gripped the bottom of his dick like a blunt with her thumb and index finger because his penis was too small to palm with her hands. She went down and placed her mouth on his dick and began sucking. 10 strokes and 30 seconds later the trick came. *Bingo! wish I could say that was a first but it wasn't,* Green Eyes thought to herself. In her world this was the norm. 60 seconds or less, easy money. And she wouldn't want it any other way.

------$$$$------

Boom!!!

The hotel door kicks in and fly open like a police swat team was raiding the place. Jackpot jumped up and leaped like a Jack in the box to his feet only to be knocked down by a blunt object to his head. Dazed and confused he began to realize what happened as his eyes focused and vision became clearer. Payday had busted in his room catching him slipping and off guard, then hit him with the butt of his gun.

"Yeah nigga, I told you I'd be seeing you." Payday spoke in a told you so type way. Jackpot had a gash on his head leaking blood like a faucet and was still seeing stars. Payday closed the hotel room door and continued to speak. "Wuss craccin Cuzz, oh wait...should I say, pimpin? Yeah wuss up wit all dat slick shit now? What, cat got cha tongue? Don't tell me the pimp is lost for words. I mean, you said we could get into some gangsta shit, right?

Payday cocked back the nina and pointed the weapon in the direction of Jackpot, who was on the floor next to the bed on half his side, bleeding like a pig. "Nigga where your stash at?" Payday asked, looking serious as Dough Boy in Boyz n the Hood when he went to avenge his brothers death.

"Why you doing this? We pose ta be pimps. What part of the game is this? Jackpot pleaded to no avail. "Nigga you knew what it was that night. I told you, I didn't give a fuck about your pimpin, but you thought I was playing. You thought it was a joke. Well tell me something...do you think I'm joking now? Payday asked, grinning with an evil smile like the Joker in Bat Man. "So you saying you gon kill me over a bitch?"

"Only if you don't do what the fuck I say. Now first and foremost...where's your muh fuckin stash? I ain't gonna ask you again nigga. Next time I'm ah let my bitch Nina do the talking," Payday said, still pointing the 9 in Jackpot's face. Jackpot knew he couldn't give up his stash. Not for the fear of giving up his money, but because he felt like once he did, he was a dead man. There was no way Payday was gonna let him live after this. Too much had happened.

Jackpot knew his only chance was to get that mutha fuckin gun out his hand, then it was on. *Think fast Jackpot think!* Jackpot thought to himself as he tried to figure out what his next move would be. At that moment, Yuki walked in which caught Payday off guard and threw him by surprise. That split second that Payday took his eyes off Jackpot and towards Yuki was all the time Jackpot needed to make his move. Jackpot grabbed the barrel of the 9 as it went off inches from his face. The loud firecracker like bang left Jackpot's ears ringing and Yuki screaming. As Payday and Jackpot wrestled with the 9, Yuki looked for a way to help her folks.

By this time, the hotel manager had already called the police after the 1st shot was fired and heard. When the 2nd shot went off, the gun was pointed towards the ceiling with both of Jackpot's hands on the barrel and Payday's on the handle and trigger. The shot through the ceiling sent a stray bullet into the room above and hit a guest in the chest while they slept. Yuki jumped on Payday's back to try and help but it only made matters worst. Payday just shrugged her off and backhand fisted her into unconsciousness, as she hit the wall and slid to the floor. At that moment, a voice had yelled, **"Freeze!"** from the doorway. Startled, Payday turned around, 9 in hand towards the entrance to find 2 police officers guns drawn with their glocks out. At that moment everything seemed to move in slow motion like the Matrix. **"Drop the weapon!"** the police ordered, but by this point, Payday felt like he had nothing to lose. With his gun still raised, he tried to squeeze off a shot but was denied, as he was cut down by a hail of bullets. Payday never had a chance. He was dead before his bullet riddled body hit the floor.

------$$$$------

Jackpot and Yuki was brought in for questioning and then released, see and how the evidence pointed to a break in, attempted robbery, and assault. The police questioned Jackpot for 3 hours after he got out of the hospital to stitch the large gash that was in his head. Yuki was still shook up from the whole ordeal. Green Eyes was blowing Jackpot's pager up, every since she came back to the hotel earlier that night to find, the door kicked in, police, and yellow tape. She still didn't have a clue as to what went down and was scared to death. She prayed her family was alright. Just as her brain would began to think the worst, her pager went off. It was Jackpot. *Thank god!* she thought to herself, after calling back the number and speaking with her folks. Jackpot told Green Eyes he would meet her back at the hotel and explain everything when he got there. Also, they was leaving San Francisco... **TONIGHT!**

12 OAKLAND CALIFORNIA

It's been three weeks since the tragic ordeal that took place in San Francisco. Since then, Jackpot and his hoes have been in Oakland. Home of the true Macks. In the little bit of time that Jackpot's been in Oakland, he managed to stack up $22,000. The situation that transpired in Frisco taught Jackpot one thing, actually 2. Stay sucka free, because everyone that claims to be a pimp isn't always as such, and send money home from time to time incase you get robbed.

So now Jackpot was sending money back to his momma's house in all sorts of ways. From travelers checks, western union, to straight cash stuffed into a teddy bear disguised as a gift for a child. As his money got longer, he found more creative ways to transport the loot. Like buying a rare expensive coin in one state or city, then trading it in and reselling it back to a coin dealer back home for the same value. He would do this with coins, stamps, and loose diamonds because the value always stayed the same and never decreased. So unlike cars, electronics and junk jewelry, these items "never" depreciated in value after you bought them. He would do this with anything over $10,000 to stay one up on the FEDS, and off their radar. Also, if someone ever tried to rob him, who was gonna notice the rare limited edition 1912 silver coin worth over $35,000?

Jackpot was sharp like that. When he was young his momma would always say, "learn from your mistakes, and fool me once...shame on you, fool me twice...shame on me!" This was advice Jackpot always took to heart. So you may catch him slipping once, but never twice. And he lived by that.

Jackpot met a lot of macks and players while in Oakland. This is where he started to make a real name for himself. He had knocked a new hoe from this player name "Mackadamian," 2 weeks after arriving in the town. The bitch was black, but she was a go getta. Not to mention, she had natural long silky hair to her shoulders, light brown complexion, and a smile that lit up the room when she walked in. Because so, Jackpot named her "Sunshine." Sunshine was the only dark skin black hoe he knew that got money like a white girl.

Maybe it was her flawless smooth skin. Maybe it was her natural DD titties. Maybe it was her big firm apple bottom ass. Or maybe it was just the way she talked to, and finessed a trick out of his shit. Tricks were like putty in her hands. She was born to be a hoe. She loved everything about the game and now, she belonged to Jackpot. Jackpot road on the track. Up and down MacArthur Blvd. searching for fresh meat. He was now 3 deep with no sleep, over 50 grand in his stack, and being recognized as a real cross country mack. Life was good. Jackpot turned up the volume on the car stereo and bumped the sounds of Too Short's, "Ain't Nothing Like Pimping" track.

Between the money Jackpot started out with before he hit the road, and what he accumulated since then to add with it, had Jackpot feeling like a rich man. He had made a trip back home one weekend while he left his hoes on automatic (hoe'n on their own) to get his finances in order and bring some of the money he made on the road back home to put up in his safe. First thing he did when he came home was found a bails bondsman and gave him $10,000. That was "get out of jail free" money, just incase him or one of his hoes ever got locked up.

Then he found a good lawyer and gave him a $20,000 retainer. Also, just incase. Then with his last $20,000 he placed it in a water proof coffee can and buried it on the side of his momma's house by the lemon tree. This left Jackpot with nothing but 3 hoes and a rental, but he was happy because he knew he had secured his future. He felt safe, and he would make all that back in no time.

While other pimps was blowing their money on jewelry and fancy cars, Jackpot was putting his away for a rainy day. And now that the possible storm was covered...shit, more than covered. He could now sit back and enjoy the money he made from here on out. Jackpot told himself that he was going back to Oakland, stay a couple more weeks, and then continue going cross country until he hit every major track in the U.S. Then he was gonna come home, buy his house, and floss like a mutha fucka. He had it all mapped out. And with that in mind, he went back to Oakland.

------$$$$------

Jackpot pulled over to the side of the curb where he saw Sunshine standing. She had just gotten out of a tricks car from pulling a date no sooner than Jackpot pulled up. Sunshine was looking sexy in some daisy duke shorts, cut off shirt revealing her stomach, and hoe shoes. Her hair was pressed and fell down passed her shoulders. Sunshine was a straight dime piece.

"Sup bitch, how's business?" Jackpot asked, speaking through the passenger side window slightly leaned over and perched on his right arm while the car still idled.

"Kinda slow Daddy, but I'm still making it work. I got $350 so far, and another trick on his way back from the bank, he had to get some more money from the ATM. If that goes through that'll be another $100. Either way I'm a make my quota tonight Daddy," Sunshine said, with every bit of confidence that she'd do just that. Jackpot broke Sunshine for the $350 and told her to stay down. Before taking off he asked if she had seen her wife-n-law Yuki. She told him, "yeah like 20 minutes ago pulling a date." He said alright and to page him if she needed anything. She said alright then ran to a tricks car that was waiting at the corner and jumped in like she already knew him. *Must be the date she was waiting on and talking about earlier,* Jackpot thought to himself as he drove off and headed back to his hotel room to relax and chill, until his bitches got off work and home with his money. Oakland was slower than San Francisco, and even slower than Hollywood, at least as far as the money went. A hoe here average $500 to $700 a night. But what this track lacked in money, it made up for in game.

Pimps in Oakland had a slick tongue. Mouth piece is what they called it. These was some trendsetters. 70% of all the street slang in america came out of Oakland. Shit, this is where they filmed The Mack. A pimp cult classic.

If your game wasn't trump tight and you set a bitch down on "this" track, it was a high percentage that you was gonna get knocked and have news served to you before you could double back. This was also the home of the gorillas.

A nigga here would throw a bitch in the trunk in a heartbeat. Have the hoe in a unfamiliar town whether she like it or not, putting the pimpin down in a real way. This was the land of the Macks. Masters at Applying Correct Knowledge.

This was where Jackpot would get and keep his game razor sharp. One thing Jackpot liked about Oakland was, there was no gang banging like in L.A. or San Diego. There was still a gangsta element, but nothing in comparison to the mean streets of southern California.

In Oakland they rep blocks, like in New York. Oakland was about their money. They wasn't killing over colors unless the color was green...money green! Jackpot stopped at a red light on his way back to the hotel. A candy apple red mustang 5.0 with match box tires and gold Daytons pulled up on the side of him. The windows was tinted but the front driver and passenger side windows were rolled down. The 2000 watt system shook the mirrors in Jackpot's car. He could feel the bass in his chest, even before the car came to a complete stop. Jackpot and the driver of the 5.0 made eye contact and looked at each other like they had saw one another some place before. They both had that look like they couldn't place the face. The occupant in the 5.0 nodded like, "wuss up?" Jackpot equally nodded back. The light turned green and the 5.0 took off first. As Jackpot took his foot off the brake and gave the car some gas, all he saw left of the mustang was it's license plate, which said...**F.A.B**

------$$$$------

Beep beep...beep beep, 1602

Yuki's pager went off. "Daddy's paging me," Yuki said to her wife-n-law Green Eyes as she examined the numbers on her pager. "He probably just checking up on us. Let me go call him back and see what he wants. I'll be right back girl."

"Okay, I'm a see if I can turn a quick date before we take it in and call it a night."

"Alright wifey, I'll be right back." Yuki went to call her folks while Green Eyes stayed behind to pull one last possible date. She had made $450 and didn't like coming in short. She prided herself for always coming in with her quota and not a penny short. She knew, she was only 1 date away from fulfilling her obligations. So with that in mind, she stayed behind.

Damn, Daddy didn't even leave the number to the hotel room or where he at, just his code number, Yuki thought to herself, just as her pager went off again, with a seven digit number and Jackpot's secret code as if JP was reading her mind or something. Yuki dialed the number on her pager and waited for her folks to answer.

"Holiday Inn, may I help you?" a female voice responded on the other end throwing Yuki off for a split second. "Um, yeah may I have room 226 please?"

"Yes, one minute please while I connect you." Three seconds into the elevator music and Jackpot answered the phone.

------$$$$------

"Wuss up bitch? Holla at a pimp!" the voice from the red 5.0 said to Green Eyes on the corner standing alone. Green Eyes immediately put her head down towards the ground, turned around and walked away in the opposite direction.

The pimp got out the car and began to follow her spittin his pimpin in a, "I'm not taking no for an answer" type of way. "Bitch, you can run but you can't hide. Pimpin gon be on you like that raggedy coat you're wearing. Hoe let me take you to the big leagues like the Oakland A's. I got conversation if you got motivation. Hoe up or blow up bitch, you're in the presence of a pimp! Choose or lose. Make your next move, be your best move, cuz pimpin ready ta serve some news." Green Eyes just kept on walking with her head down making sure as to not make any type of eye contact or say something that would cause her to be outta pocket with him.

By this time, the pimp was on her heels like a shadow in the night. She could feel his hot breath on the back of her neck when he spoke. Green Eyes tried to cross the street to get away but was to no avail. He followed her. He wasn't letting up. He was a pimp on a mission and his mission was to knock this hoe. "Who's your folks bitch? cuz if you're out here renegadin, then I'm about to start regulating," the pimp said, ready to break this hoe for all she had. The pimp grabbed Green Eyes left arm and spun her around. Now they were eye to eye.

"My folks is Jackpot," Green Eyes said, realizing at this point she had no other choice but to speak. As soon as the pimp spun her around, he immediately recognized her.

Oh shit, this is Payday's ex hoe. "Break yo self hoe. Bitch, you outta pocket!" the pimp went through Green Eyes pockets, purse, and bra before he found her money. This was the first time Green Eyes was ever caught slipping. She usually had her money hidden in her pussy, but since she was trying to pull a date, she had it out her pussy and in her bra.

"Yeah hoe, that's wut I'm talkin bout. Put 6 mo wit dat and you can come home. This is Fuk-A-Bitch Tha Pimp!"

------$$$$------

"Hey Daddy," Yuki said, speaking to her folks on the phone.

"Wuss up, I was paging to see if you and your wifey's was about done. A pimp was just checkin the time and realized it was kinda late."

"Yeah I'm done, I made my quota. I'm just waiting on Green Eyes to finish up, then we're coming home. She said she wanted to pull 1 more date while I called you. She should be done now."

"What about Sunshine?"

"I saw her earlier. She said she had a regular that was coming to pick her up and spend $500 just to spend the rest of the day with him. She said he sees her every friday. She said she'd meet us back at the hotel when she was done."

"Alright, sounds good. Then I'll see ya'll when ya'll get home." Jackpot hung up the phone and sparked a blunt, sat back and waited for his hoes.

Yuki went back to the track where she left Green Eyes minutes earlier to find her visibly shook up. Yuki asked her wifey what was wrong and why she was crying. Green Eyes explained to her what had happened and took place moments earlier before Yuki arrived. Green Eyes knew, coming in the house empty handed was a no no and her folks would be hella pissed.

"But you didn't do anything wrong," Yuki said, trying to comfort her wifey in response to Green Eyes telling her she felt like Jackpot was gonna kick her ass for getting, "broke" and not coming home with any money. The worst thing a hoe could do was come home after being out all day with no money.

"I'm sure Daddy a understand. Come on, let's go home." Yuki said, sounding sure of herself. But Green Eyes wasn't as convinced.

------$$$$------

Jackpot answered the door from the knock of a delicate woman's touch to find Sunshine before him. She smiled with that radiant glow that a hoe has only after making a shit load of cash. She greeted her Daddy with money in hand and a kiss on the cheek. Jackpot took the money and playfully tapped her on the ass, as she walked pass and came inside. Sunshine kicked off her Steve Madden heels and sat on the bed while Jackpot counted the money she just handed him. She made $850 which was good for Oakland and great for a black bitch. Sunshine's sugar daddy coming through is what put her over the top. "Damn girl, you're killin em out there." Sunshine just smiled, happy to have pleased her folks like a proud daughter handing her father a report card full of A's. "I'm proud of you girl, good job."

"Thank you Daddy." Sunshine hopped up off the bed, gave her folks a hug, and then got in the shower to wash the trick aftershave and cheap cologne smell off that all hoes have on them after a long night of hoe'n. *1 down, 2 ta go,* Jackpot thought to himself, as he glanced down at his watch to check the time. 20 minutes later, Sunshine was done with her shower and drying off, when her wife-n-laws walked in. Jackpot could tell right away by the expressions on their faces that something was wrong. Yuki handed Jackpot a wad of cash, sat down on the bed behind her folks and faced his back.

Green Eyes said that she needed to speak to him, not wanting to talk about what had happened in front of her wife-n-laws for lack of not knowing how Jackpot would react, and embarrassed for coming home empty handed. Jackpot sensed and picked up on the fact and told her..."Let's go outside and talk."

Green Eyes told her folks everything that had happened. The entire story from beginning to end. Jackpot got upset. Not at his bitch, but the nigga that violated the game. If everything played out like Green Eyes said it did, then that nigga had "no" reason to place his bitch under pimp arrest. But then again, what if the hoe was lying and "taking him places?" (running game on him). *But why would she?* he thought to himself. She never put herself in a situation to be outta pocket before. He had to play this smart because he also knew his other 2 hoes was watching. The way he did or didn't react could effect a lot. "What was the pimps name?" he asked her.

"Fuk-a-bitch." Jackpot had heard the name before, think he might have even saw the pimp before in passing. Jackpot also figured he was from Oakland, when Green Eyes told him that he had a full set of gold teeth in his mouth. Those were the only Cali niggas that got down like that. Jackpot's instincts told him he was from Oakland, and Jackpot knew how Oakland nigga's played.

"Alright bitch check this out. You're not new to this and you've always been true to this so I'm a stall you out. I ain't gonna trip unless I talk to this nigga and hear a different ending to the same movie. You know I don't trust a bitch as far as I can throw the hoe, but I do trust you, about 1%. Like the bible says, the size of a mustard seed is about how much faith I have in you to tell the truth, and every other bitch in this stable for that matter.

"So I'm a give you the benefit of the doubt this time and let shit slide, but if you ever come in here without my money again, you can best believe I'm a send your ass right back to the track and get my cheese. Whether it was your fault or not. I don't give a fuck...hoe smarter! This ain't baseball so you don't get 3 strikes. You get 1, and you just used it. So next time, if there is a next time, I suggest you hide your money better, keep it moving quicker, or stay your ass out until you make my money back. Bitch you got that?"

"Yes Daddy, I'm sorry. It won't happen again," Green Eyes responded, like it was her fault that it happened in the first place. Jackpot knew, that more than likely the situation happened and went down exactly how she said it did, but if he would have just took her word and let her off the hook, then one day she could lie and come in with the same story.

Jackpot wasn't about to let his hoes start "taking him places. Believing any and everything a hoe say was a sure fire way to have her stealing and hiding money from you in the future. That's also when a bitch a get lazy and start talking about how slow it was when really, she was ho'cializing, Fucking off, bullshitting and wasting time.

Jackpot also knew that, he couldn't be too hard on the bitch because it could very well effect his money and bring a dark cloud amongst his stable, and with things moving ever so sweet lately, he didn't need that. Like he always said, "a happy hoe, was a good hoe" and he wasn't about to have bitches walking around tripping with their lips poked out. "Go inside and relax Babe, tomorrow's another day."

"Okay Daddy," Green Eyes answered, then walked inside as Jackpot thought about something Trust had told him. "Beat em down, then build em up." And that's exactly what Jackpot just did. Damn, Trust would be proud.

2 weeks later...

"Alright bitches, we been putting it down on these Oakland streets for about 2 months, give or take a couple weeks. What ever the timeline, we been here long enough and I'm ready to hit the road. Actually...I'm ready to get out of Cali." Jackpot spoke as the hoes eyes grew big as a cartoon character surprised on crystal meth. None of the hoes been out of California, other than Arizona, which they all felt didn't count. Out there it was hot, ghetto, and filled with a bunch of black hoes on the track that loved to hate. Phoenix Arizona. Jackpot continued talking. "Pack it up bitches. Next stop...Seattle Washington."

13 $EATTLE WASHINGTON

It's been 2 days since Jackpot and his bitches arrived in Seattle. Jackpot loved the city, minus all the fuckin rain and cold weather. Once a Cali nigga leaves California to explore new regions or lay his head down somewhere else, the first thing he has to get use to is the climate change.

No more year round sun. No more tank tops in the winter. *Yo, what is that, snow?* Yeah, that's the hardest part about leaving Cali. But other than that, Seattle was the shit. Reason being, Because Jackpot never saw so many snow bunnies in his life. Even on the sandy beaches of California.

Another good thing about the white bitches here was, pimps was knocking these hoes left and right. Jackpot knew, as long as he stayed down he had ta come up. For the next few days, Jackpot put his pimp campaign down tough. Every day, every night. He was determined to knock his 4th hoe. When his bitches was on the track working, Jackpot was on the track searching. By the 2nd week, all the hard work had payed off. One day, Jackpot was checking out the local Greyhound station for runaways and renegades. Now a renegade is a bitch that hoes for herself and doesn't have a pimp. A runaway is a hoe that just up and left her folks one day out of the blue.

The bus station was the best place to find these bitches. One day when Jackpot was making his daily rounds through the Greyhound bus station like he did every day, he ran into a girl name Lisa. Lisa was a 23 year old white girl from Ohio. She had just gotten out of prison for transporting weed when she was 18. Story has it, her man was a big time dope dealer in Ohio. One day, he asked her to drive a car across state with some work in the trunk. He assured her that she'd be safe because she was white and looked square as a box of Cheerios. Her young naive mind and love for him, made her not even give it a second thought.

Little did she know that the FEDS had been watching her man for quite some time now and was beginning to close in. Not even 12 miles into her trip, she got pulled over and arrested for possession with intent, and transporting. The FEDS knew she was just a mule and wanted her man. They figured they could get her to flip on him and put him away forever. When she refused to talk and give him up, they charged her with the stuff and gave her 6 years with 85%. Now she was fresh out, at the bus station, and nowhere to go.

Lisa was slim, only weighed about 120 pounds soaking wet with cement shoes on and weights around her neck. Typical white girl body. No butt, medium size tits, long hair with a cute face. Just how the tricks love em. She had long curly blond hair to her waist, which was the first thing Jackpot noticed when he saw her. Real tight curls like she had a perm, but hers were all natural. She had milk skin complexion like she grew up somewhere with very little sun, or spent most of her time locked up indoors. She was naturally cute but with a little make-up she'd look exotic. She had nice eyes and full lips. Jackpot noticed those right away also.

Another thing Jackpot would come to respect and admire about Lisa was the fact that she didn't snitch on her ex and rode the beef like a soldier. *Shit, if more "niggas" was like that today.* When Jackpot first approached Lisa, she asked if he was a pimp. That threw him off for a second because he was actually trying to down play the fact, knowing that she wasn't a hoe or in the life. So he felt like he had to treat her like a fresh turn out until the time was right to spring the pimpin out the box.

Between having a black drug dealer as her ex, and doing time in prison, Lisa was a lot smarter than she looked. She came across as an average white girl you'd see every day on any giving street in america. But in actuality, she had game. And everyone knows, game recognize game. So Jackpot responded as such, "why, you looking for one?"

"Actually, I'm not 'looking' for anything, but maybe a new shot at life." Lisa responded back, playing verbal tennis with Jackpot, with a look on her face like...your serve.

"Oh is dat right? I can dig it. So what type of life are you running from?"

"Who said I was running?"

"Well you said you was looking for a new shot at life which can only happen if you leave your old one behind."

"True, but running and looking is 2 different things. You see my old life as I knew it is over. So at this point and time I'm in transition and looking for something new. But you know, you never did answer my question."

"And what's that?" Jackpot asked, playing dumb while already knowing the answer.

"Are you a pimp?"

"What if I was?"

"Oh, so now you're answering a question with a question huh? Well I'll just take that as a yes then." *Oh this bitch thinks she's smart,* Jackpot thought to himself. "I'm a gentleman of leisure Babygirl."

"Yeah like I said, a pimp!" *Oh yeah, this bitch is too smart for her own damn good.* Jackpot let out a slight laugh and said, "would it bother you if I was?"

"No, not really. The only thing that bothers me is if a man can't be honest. If you're a pimp, then say you're a pimp. If not, then not."

"I can respect that. You're pretty outspoken, I like that. You don't seem like the kind of girl that bites her tongue much."

"No, I always speak my mind. Sometimes it gets me in trouble." They both laughed.

"I bet. Well pretty lady, My name's Jackpot but some call me JP for short." Jackpot stuck out his hand, she stuck out hers, shook it and said, "I'm Lisa." And that was how they met.

Lisa wasn't a hoe, so Jackpot had to teach her everything she needed to know. At the time they met, Jackpot didn't realize that Lisa actually had dreams of being a porn star. Shit, being a porn star was the cousin to hoe'n. So once Jackpot found that out, he knew it would be no sweat turning her out, or as Jackpot like to say...turning her on, to some "game." Jackpot spent a lot of time with Lisa, prepping and getting her ready for her new shot at life. He didn't bring her around his other hoes right away because at the moment, that would have been a conflict of interest since Lisa wasn't a hoe yet.

His bitches would have more than likely tripped off the fact that he was spending time with a square bitch and started acting funny. They would have felt like their folks was trickin on the bitch. Something hoes hated more than anything. It was hard for a hoe to put up with that. Especially when you have some of these sucka fa love ass pimp niggas with a hoe and a wife.

The hoe makes money and the wife or so called girlfriend sit back and spends it. That gives the game a black eye because any true pimp or hoe knows...what's good for your hoe, is good for your girlfriend or wife. Period! But sometimes, hoes don't understand the prepping process. They don't realize that you have to spend money to make money. They think Rome was built in a day. They forget about when they were new to the game and what it took to get them hoe'n.

See some bitches are hoes by nature and some aren't. The ones that aren't, is gonna take a lot more prepping to put in the game. Every bitch wasn't touched by her daddy or uncle when she was young. Every hoe isn't chasing or trying to feed a drug habit. Every bitch isn't a nympho. So every bitch just can't be turned out in a day.

Jackpot knew this, and knowing so, if a bitch wasn't a hoe already, then he took his time turning her out. The flip side of the coin was, Jackpot knew that a lot of bitches was holding on to baggage from previous and past relationships that they still hadn't let go of. A lot of women was bruised inside.

Some still held a lot of contempt in their heart. Jealousy, envy and larceny. That type of bitch could do a lot of damage. She was the type that could wipe out what it took years to build in minutes. She could fuck up a whole stable in seconds. She was poison. And one thing about poison is...sometimes you don't know it's poison until it's too late. Jackpot tried his hardest not to bring this type a bitch into his circle and for the most part, up until now had done good. But like the bible says, the devil comes in all forms, and little did Jackpot know it at the time, but Lisa was the Devil!

------$$$$------

After Jackpot and Lisa hit it off at the bus station, Jackpot convinced her not to get on the bus and give him a try at life. If it didn't work out, he'd get her another ticket to anywhere she wanna go, personally. Lisa felt like, what did she have to lose? and left with him. For the next 2 weeks, Jackpot spent every day prepping Lisa and making sure she had what it took to join his stable.

If Jackpot was still new to the game or didn't already have 3 hoes working, he probably would have turned her out sooner. But Jackpot knew he didn't need to rush, so he didn't. He took his time. Once they left the bus station, Jackpot set Lisa up in a nice hotel of her own away from his other bitches.

He picked her brain about any and everything and got to know her. Trust taught Jackpot that a good pimp knows how to talk, but a great pimp knows how to listen. If a mutha fucka shut up for a second, sit back and listen, then a bitch a spill her whole life story to you. Her likes, her dislikes, ambitions, goals, what she want or expects out of life. The whole nine yards. One has to remember, a female likes to talk by nature. This is why they can spend hours on the phone with their homegirls gossiping about bullshit. So after checking Lisa into her room and dropping off her stuff, Jackpot took her out to eat and talk.

Jackpot took Lisa out to T.G.I FRIDAYS which was his favorite restaurant, and got a dim lit booth in the back away from customers. Jackpot ordered his usual Jack Daniel's steak, medium well, with mash potatoes and cream broccoli. Lisa ordered what most females ordered, chicken alfredo and salad. While the two waited for their food to arrive, they talked. This was when Jackpot learned about Lisa's past and her just getting out of prison. This is where he also learned about Lisa's dreams of being a porn star. Lisa was like an open book. She didn't leave nothing out, and Jackpot just sat and listened. After eating their meal and talking for 2 hours, Jackpot summoned the waitress over for their check, paid the tab, left a tip, and bounced.

Jackpot liked Lisa because she looked square as a box but could be sly as a fox. She had a girl next door look and way about her. She wasn't as attractive as Jackpot's other 3 bitches, but she was still more than pretty enough to turn a few heads or 2. You could look in her face and tell she'd been through some things in life. Especially when you looked in her eyes. Jackpot always felt like the eyes were the window to the soul. Your body language and face could always hide what your eyes couldn't. When Jackpot looked into Lisa's eyes, he saw heart ache, pain, and trust issues. This was the first sign that Jackpot should have walked away and never looked back, but he didn't. And little did he know that one day it would cost him his freedom.

Jackpot drove Lisa back to her hotel. On the way there, he thought about everything they'd talked about. He was still surprised that she had spent 5 years in prison. Apparently the way it went down, she was suppose to meet a guy in Seattle, who would give her a car already loaded with drugs in the trunk hidden in a spare tire, then drive the car and drugs back to ohio.

Needless to say, she never made it. Jackpot felt like she was gangsta for not snitching when he knew that most females in her shoes would've. Especially when the dude she was messing with cut her off immediately after her arrest. He even stopped excepting her collect calls from the county jail and prison. And this was suppose to be the love of her life. The man she would die for. Shit, the man she would lay down and do time for! This is where she developed trust issues. That very moment, she stopped living for others, and started living for herself.

------$$$$------

2 weeks after spending time with Lisa, getting to know her, her getting to know him, as well as putting her up on all the ins and outs of the game. He felt like he was ready to bring her home and introduce her to her wife-n-laws. He kept it real with her from day one. He never hid the fact that he had other hoes. He never told her, or had her to believe that she would be the only one. Jackpot knew that playing that game was like walking a fire lit tight rope with gasoline shoes on. Jackpot prided

himself in always keeping it real. This was a game about choices. So if you chose to be with him then you except him as he was. Plus, he was "never" gonna give a bitch the satisfaction of saying he lied to, or tricked her into being with him. *Fuck that! You knew what it was when you met me.* That was Jackpot's favorite line. How could a bitch turn around in the end and flip the script when he laid all his cards on the table for her to see? Shit, you can't play 3 Card Monte with the suits showing. So Jackpot made sure Lisa knew exactly what she was getting into before he brung her home. Truth be told, Lisa seemed excited about joining the family. It was like a new adventure for her. The only thing about adventures though, is they don't last forever. The day before Jackpot brung Lisa home, he sat his other hoes down and told them that he had a new bitch that was gonna join the family. He explained to them how he met her, and what she was all about. He told them to make sure they make her feel welcome within her new family when he brung her home. The hoes agreed and couldn't wait to meet their new wife–n–law.

------$$$$------

Jackpot walked into the hotel room that Green Eyes, Yuki, and Sunshine was staying at. Lisa walked in following behind Jackpot, slightly nervous not really sure what to expect. Sure Jackpot told her everything would be cool, but Lisa knew first hand how catty women could be, especially if they felt threatened. But to Lisa's surprise, they weren't the ones threatened at all, she was. *My god they're so beautiful*, Lisa thought to herself. The girls all introduced themselves, shook her hand, and gave her a hug. Lisa had to admit, the girls made her feel real welcome. Jackpot smiled inside, proud of how the whole scene went down, watching his hoes interact and get acquainted with one another. He couldn't help but to think about how much more money he was about to make.

For the next few weeks they stayed in Seattle getting money. Lisa took to hoe'n like a fish to water. She got along with her wifey's too. They were like 4 sisters. Actually, they were like 4 lovers. All of the women were bisexual, so with or without Jackpot in the picture, The late night freak sessions was something that a make Heather Hunter blush.

Life was great. Money was flowing in by the stacks, hoes was happy, and Jackpot was coming up quicker than a hot air balloon with rocket boosters. Shit was good. But, as we know...all good things must eventually come to an end.

14 NEW MILLENNIUM

1999...4 years later.

"3...2...1...Happy New Year!!!" It was the end of the 90's and the end of an era as we knew it. The world was scared that the computers would shut down and life as we knew it would dramatically change. Well, they was 1/2 right. Jackpot had been through a lot in 4 years. He'd touched every track and back, at least twice. From west to east, north to south. From the big apple to the pineapple.

Jackpot did what he set out to do. To become the biggest cross country pimp to ever live. He still had his same 4 hoes as well as a few stragglers spread out throughout the states. Throughout his 4 year journey, many hoes came and went. That was the name of the game, cop-n-blow. But not his main 4. Yuki, Green Eyes, Sunshine and Lisa. They were with him to the fullest. In it for the long haul. They loved Jackpot to death. "Till Game Do Us Part" they would say. And they took that shit to heart. Especially Lisa. She had grown to be obsessed with Jackpot and it was beginning to cause problems between the other hoes. Lisa started to distance herself from the others. She started acting like she wanted Jackpot all to herself. She started to get jealous of the other hoes because they were much younger and a lot prettier. Her heart began to grow full of envy and larceny. She hated how close Yuki and Jackpot was. She always felt like she was in competition with Yuki. If Yuki bought a nice smelling perfume, then Lisa would go out and buy the same for herself. And after 3 years of this type of behavior, the shit was finally coming to a head. It was a new millennium. The clocks didn't stop, the world didn't end. The hoes kept choosing, and the pimps kept pimpin.

The first year of Jackpot's pimp career was the year he made his mark in the game. He did everything he set out to do, and then some. He bought a house in Bonita. A nice big 7 bedroom, 4 bath, 3 car garage, mini mansion with a pool and jacuzzi in the backyard. He had 2 palm trees and 4 fruit trees that sat in his backyard. The back lawn was big enough to play football on.

The house was 3 levels. When you walked in the front door, you was on the second floor, at which time you had the option of going up or downstairs. Upstairs was where the bedrooms was located. The master bedroom was big enough to fit 3 full size automobiles inside. It had its own bathroom with a jacuzzi oval shaped tub and heated tile floors. All the fixtures were gold plated. The walk in closet was the size of an average persons master bedroom. Of course this was Jackpot's room. He had a big custom made circle shape bed that sat in the middle of the room with a custom persian dollar sign bed spread. He had a sony 55" inch big screen TV with surround sound to set it off. In his closet, he had tailor made Italian suits and Mauri gators in every style and color.

He had Gucci and Prada sneakers that was between $600 and $900 a piece. He had mid and full length furs, from mink to chinchillas with the matching hat. His jewelry case sat above his custom shoe rack. He had a custom made neck piece. A 24 karat 410 gram barrel chain with a 5x5 inch name plate which said Jackpot, rainbow curved above a slot machine showing 3 sevens. Flooded with 20 karats worth of flawless canary yellow and white diamonds. He had a Cartier Tic Tac Toe watch with the bezel iced out. Custom diamond earrings that said Jackpot. Fat pinky ring of a crown flooded with diamonds and a 3 row canary yellow diamond bracelet to match his chain.

The next 4 bedrooms was on the opposite side of the hall on the other end of the house. Those was his hoe's rooms. There was 2 more rooms downstairs, one with its own bathroom. That was the guest room. He made the other room an office. The house had 2 living rooms. 1 on the 2nd floor and one on the 1st. Both rooms decked out with top of the line furniture.

The kitchen was huge, with an island counter in the middle of it. This was Jackpot's dream house. It cost him $940,000. He put it in his mothers name and put down the bank required 10%. By the 2nd year they all had cars. Jackpot had a 1998 600 Mercedes Benz, big body. He had it a year before it even hit the streets. He still kept the 510 wagon his mother gave him because it held sentimental value.

The hoes all had matching 535 BMW's. Jackpot bought them all the same car, that way they couldn't fuss or fight about who's was better. Same way you do when you have kids. Buy one candy, you have to get em all candy.

The hoes didn't shop at Macy's or JC Penny's anymore. Now they shopped at Saks and Neiman Marcus. They no longer went to Plaza Bonita. Now it was Horton Plaza and Fashion Valley. In 2 years they had truly came up. In 4 years they were ballin outta control. Jackpot felt on top of the world, and now it was New Years. Time for celebration. Vegas was packed. Millions of people walked the streets in anticipation as the count down took place outside on the MGM Grands jumbo screen. The streets was closed off like time square. Couples, friends, and love ones held each other close. In vegas, you can drink alcohol on the streets so drinks was raised in the air.

Jackpot sat with his 4 hoes proud, thinking about his accomplishments and how far they've come together. His hoes was thinking the same thing. After the countdown, they kissed, gambled, and partied the night away. Everything was lavish. From the penthouse Luxor suite they stayed in, to the endless bottles of Cristal they popped. They did Vegas in style. Everywhere they went they turned heads. It was a long road but they definitely arrived. This would be a night that represents change. For better or worst. Good or bad. And truth be told, after that night, that's exactly what happened. Things changed.

------$$$$------

"Okay listen up, this piece of shit is a known pimp. We know this because, I've been watching him every since his brother A-$ki was killed. His brother was a low life gang banger from Skyline East Side Piru." The detective known as Spyder briefed his men. "I know that the apple doesn't fall too far from the tree. So I knew it a only be a matter of time before he too, ended up in a life of crime.

"Me and my partner Brittle have been keeping close tabs on him every since he graduated from high school. He fell off our radar for about a year or so then popped back up in 97. I've been on his ass every since." Detective Spyder was a gang detective wannabe know it all cop from San Diego, that for some reason, made it his life long mission to take down Jackpot at any cost. He even put off his retirement 3 times to do so.

When Jackpot was still a teenager, Spyder was head of gang detail in South East. He hated Jackpot for the life his brother use to live before he was shot and killed by a rival gang. Spyder knew and was well aware of how active A-$ki was, but could never pin anything on him or catch him in the act of committing a crime.

He hated the fact that A-$ki always stayed 1 step ahead of him. Like when Spyder would pull $ki and his friends over for D.W.B (Driving While Black) and find nothing, only to find out later that a group of people matching their description earlier was involved in a drive-by shooting. Since this was the 80's, and not the snitching late 90's or 2000, most people kept their mouths shut. Even when it was the so called victim being brought in to point out the shooter in a line up. Back then niggas lived by a code of, what happens in the streets, gets handled in the streets. So even though $ki may have had a lot of close calls, Spyder was never able to catch him slippin. And just when he thought he was close, someone killed him. So after $ki's death, detective Spyder drew his attention to his younger brother Ricky. Jackpot was 4 years younger than his brother. Spyder was the reason Jackpot spent 2 years in The Arizona Boys Ranch when he was 14 for defending himself when 4 mexican gang members tried to jump him and ended up getting the worst end of the stick. Spyder was able to convince the D.A. and judge that Ricky had to have had a weapon to inflict the type of damage he laid on the mexicans. That was Jackpots 1 and only brush with the law, but not Detective Spyder. Spyder made it his mission to throw Jackpot in Juvenal Hall, Youth Authority, County Jail, and eventually...the Penitentiary, but was unsuccessful.

Now Detective Brittle was head of the San Diego Vice Squad. Jackpot came across Brittle's radar one night in 98 when he was pulled over on El Cajon Blvd. with 2 known prostitutes and a trunk full of hoe clothes. Brittle really hated pimps, because off duty he was a trick and couldn't understand why he had to pay for pussy while the pimp got it for free. He hated when he thought about his hard earned money going into a "niggers" pocket. So when he pulled Jackpot over on the blade with 2 white hoes that didn't look a day over 20, Jackpot became public enemy #1.

Brittle took Jackpot downtown for suspicion of pimping and pandering. Knowing the charges were weak and probably wouldn't stick, Brittle figured if he could separate Jackpot from his hoes, then maybe he could scare the girls and break them down into rolling over on him. But the bitches held their ground, said Jackpot was just a friend and let him go. This gave Brittle and Spyder something in common...Taking Down Jackpot!

------$$$$------

Jackpot had stepped his game up and was no longer working his hoes on the blade. He now had them in the finest escort services in town. Since making the transition, his money and profit margin grew 10 folds. His females never made less than a $1000 a night. Sometimes they made $3000 or better, and this was in San Diego, where a bitch was lucky to make her $500 quota every night on the blade. Especially now, because vice was catching on and starting to slam down hard on the track.

8th and National had dried up due to constant arrest of pimps, hoes, and tricks alike. 8th Street looked like a ghost town. In Vegas, a hoe in a escort service could easily make $3000 to $5000 a night, and for a lot less work. A lot of times, tricks just wanted to be in the company of a beautiful woman. You wasn't dealing with broke ass $50 tricks with stink dicks and no money, manners, or clue on how to treat a bitch. In the service, you came across doctors, lawyers, politicians, and powerful people with money. Especially if it was a high class escort service. Sky's the limit. This made Jackpot hood rich in a short amount of time.

While other pimps might have been 10 deep with no sleep, Jackpot had 4 go getta's that would outshine and clock in more money than all 10 hoes combined. This had other pimps hatin. They would say shit like, "keep it concrete and street." Funny thing is, now, everybody and their momma wanna throw a bitch up in the escort service. But Jackpot did it first. He did it when it wasn't the popular thing to do. When it wasn't the status quo. And that only made him get more money. Things was moving fast for Jackpot. He was averaging $5000 to $10,000 a day. His money was long and game even stronger. He was a die hard pimp knee deep in the game. The type of money he was getting would make a dope boy stand up and take notice. But as the cliché goes and Biggie said it best...mo Money, mo problems. And shit was getting hectic in Jackpot's life.

------$$$$------

"Bitch get the fuck out my face and leave me alone, I'm tryna sleep!" Lisa screamed at her wifey Yuki. "What the fuck's your problem? I just asked if you saw my purse," Yuki responded. Things had been getting really tense. Lisa had been getting into it a lot lately with the other hoes, forcing them to click up and take sides, which only made things worse, because now it gave Lisa an excuse to trip out and act like everyone was against her.

Yuki slammed Lisa's door closed as she walked away talking shit. "I hate that bitch. Fuckin trailer trash!" Yuki said to herself out loud, as Green Eyes was coming up the stairs to see what all the commotion was about. "Wuss going on up here?" Green Eyes asked.

"Same as always, Lisa's fuckin ass tripping as usual." Green Eyes rolled her eyes and shook her head like, "not again." Lisa came out the room from hearing Yuki talk about her and smacked Yuki in the face. "Now you can say I'm tripping bitch. Keep my mother fuckin name out your mouth." That was the last straw. Things had been gearing up to this very moment. The hoes been talking big shit to one another for a while now but never got physical. But once Lisa opened up Pandoras box and put her hands on Yuki, Yuki snapped. "Bitch you got me fucked up!" Yuki yelled looking meaner and more pissed off than the incredible Hulk.

Yuki lunged at Lisa swinging like a bat out of hell. She punched Lisa in the face and clawed at her eyes. Lisa grabbed and got ahold of Yuki's hair, wrapped it around her hand, and started punching her back. Green Eyes wanted to, and thought about breaking it up, but felt like Lisa needed to get her ass kicked and this was a long time coming, so she didn't. She told herself, that if Lisa starts to get the best of Yuki, "then" she'll break it up.

Yuki knew how to kick box and Lisa fought like a white girl. So even with Lisa having Yuki by the hair and semi immobile, Yuki was still fuckin her up. Yuki kicked Lisa in the stomach which made her let go of her hair. Lisa grabbed and ripped off Yuki's DKNY spaghetti strap shirt and exposed her titties which only made Yuki angrier. The hoes went at it for about 60 seconds before Green Eyes broke em up. Both bitches looked like they had been in a fight with a tiger. From that point on, things would never be the same.

------$$$$------

"Wuss up Pimp?" Jackpot answered his cellphone, driving down El Cajon Blvd. He noticed the caller ID said, "Phero" before picking up. Phero was Jackpot's high school friend. They met one day, when Phero and Jackpot was on rival break dancing crews when they were young. They had a scheduled battle between the 2 crews that was suppose to take place at the Sweetwater Skate Rink all night skate and dance function. The 2 crews went at it. It was a close battle. It came down to Phero and Jackpot. The 2 crew's best breakers. The end result was a tie. Breaking died out in Cali with Beat Street and Crush Groove and then gang bangin took over.

Phero was 2 years older than Jackpot and use to run with his brother A-$ki. After A-$ki died, Phero would come around and check on Jackpot and the family. He was cool like that. A real friend through an through and 100% loyal. This is when him and Jackpot got close.

"Wut up wit it?," Phero responded.

"Shit, just a whole lotta pimpin, you know."

"Right right. Well check this out pimp, I been fuckin wit that nigga Sammy.D, and he put me up that hoes is getting it up in DC right now in a real way."

"Yeah I was talkin to Ka$hanova and $upreme yesterday, They was sayin the same thing."

"Yeah I'm headed that way tonight, was checkin ta see if you wanna roll," Phero said.

"I don't know yet, truth be told, it might be kinda cool to flip the script and send or take one of my hoes out there. Them bitches been bad acting lately. Pimpin might need to split em up for a few weeks. Matter or fact, I may send a hoe or 2 out there on automatic. Maybe being away from me a few weeks a get these hoes some get right," Jackpot said, as he made a right and got on the I-5 south freeway to take him home.

"Alright pimp, hit me up once you decide on what you gonna do. I won't be leaving until about 12:00.""Alright playa, fa'sho." Jackpot said, then hung up the phone as he glanced in his rear view mirror and noticed that he was being followed. *Who the fuck is following me?* Jackpot thought to himself, as he got off the freeway and then merged back on just to make sure he wasn't going crazy. Sho nuff, when Jackpot got off on H Street Chula Vista, so did the car that was following him. Then when he got back on the freeway, the car that was following him did too.

"Alright, I got something for you muh fucka!" Jackpot said to himself with a tense grin, looking back at the car through his rear view mirror. *Let's see how far ya'll willing to travel,* Jackpot continued south, bypassing any and all exits that would take and lead the followers to his home. Instead, he continued driving south until he arrived at the Tijuana mexican border.

"Now if they don't follow me through I know these mutha fucka's popo cause they can't leave their jurisdiction. But if they do follow me across the border, then they're not and I'm a have to just lose em in Mexico." Jackpot said to himself, as he crossed the border. just as he thought, the car didn't follow. That's when he knew it was time to leave Daygo...Road Trip!

------$$$$------

"Hello Daddy, how was your day?" Sunshine greeted her folks as he walked in the house with her usual smile that could light up a block and signal a lost ship back to shore. "Hey Babe. kinda long, but glad to be home." Sunshine gave her folks a kiss and said, "would you like a massage or something to eat?"

"No, I'm good Babygirl. Where's your wife-n-laws at?" Before Sunshine could answer, Yuki and Lisa came from upstairs, walking downstairs towards their folks.

"Damn bitches, what the fuck happened to ya'll?" Jackpot asked, noticing the aftermath of the hoes destruction that took place earlier. Both of the bitches just stood there, heads down looking stupid.

"Don't both you bitches start talking at once. Oh now cat got cha tongue huh? Must be the same cat that got cha face. You know what, I don't even wanna hear what the fuck ya'll gotta say. The dumb ass look on ya'll faces is evident enough of what took place. Take ya'll stupid asses back upstairs to ya rooms until I'm ready ta see and talk to you."

Jackpot was hot, and he knew that he needed time to cool off before he dealt with Yuki and Lisa because if not, He might have fucked them both up himself. Lisa crossed her arms over her chest, sucked her teeth, and went to her room. Yuki gave her folks a..."it wasn't my fault, I was just defending myself" look, put her head down, and walked to her room as well. Yuki shut her door lightly, Lisa slammed hers. Another indicator of just how different these 2 bitches were.

"Where's Green Eyes at Sunshine?" Jackpot asked, taking off his Wilson leather coat and placing his car keys on the coffee table. Sunshine grabbed his coat and hung it up in the hall closet then said, "she went to go see one of her sugar daddies. She said she'll be home by 9:00."

Jackpot said alright, went downstairs to the kitchen, took a bottle of Moet out the fridge, popped the cork and poured him a glass of champagne. Sunshine rolled him a blunt and had it

143

waiting for him in the ashtray. Sunshine always did little things like that for her folks, and Jackpot loved her for it. She always knew how to make a man feel like a man and a pimp feel like a pimp.

Jackpot walked over to the custom italian leather sofa that stretched around his living room in a half circle, picked the blunt up out the ashtray that was lying on the coffee table, sat down and sparked it up. Jackpot grabbed the remote off the end table and turned on his $3,000 Sony stereo system. He then switched the mode from stereo to CD and bumped his Suga Free CD he had already pre-selected in the deck. Jackpot zoned out like a Rasta at a Marley fest as he hit the weed. Sunshine went to her room to give Jackpot some obviously much needed time to himself, as he sat back, relaxed, and figured out what his next move would be.

$$------\$\$\$\$------$$

"How the fuck did you lose him?" Detective Spyder yelled into the CB.

"We had him, but then he crossed the border into Mexico," the rookie cop responded.

"Do you think he realized he was being followed?"

"Not until he got on the freeway. When he was rolling through East San Diego he was none the wiser. But once we got on the freeway, he started driving funny. I think that's when we may have blown our cover."

"Fuck, god dammit! what kind of police work are you conducting down there? Do you need me to hold your fucking dick while you piss? If you can't handle the job let me know. This is basic police work rookie. If you're that wet behind the ears I'll get you a bib to wipe the milk off your god damn chin!"

"No Sir, I can handle the job."

"You damn hell better. Don't let him make a monkey out of you or this police department."

"I won't, I'm sure he'll be back out tomorrow on the stroll, and when I spot him I won't let him out of my site."

"I'm holding you to that rookie. Mess this up, and you'll be sharpening pencils and pushing paperwork behind a desk quicker than I can fuck my old lady, cum, and go to sleep."

------$$$$------

"Hello." Sunshine answered the house phone.

"Hello, may I speak to JP?"

"Yes, who may I say is calling?"

"Maroy."

"Okay, hold on for a sec please." Sunshine went downstairs to the living room to give her folks the phone. "Daddy, telephone."

"Who is it?" Jackpot asked, like he didn't feel like being bothered. "Maroy."

"Oh alright, bring it here." Maroy was a playalistic, underground film producer from the streets of Chicago. He ran a website called toorealfortv.com. On the site you could purchase hood DVD's about the pimp sub-culture that he had filmed and produced. The movies was a raw look into the game like no other. From watching pimps receive trophies at the International Players Ball for Pimp of the Year, to hoes getting broke on the track and pimps checking traps. If you saw

Maroy on the streets you'd think he was a pimp himself. From the tailor made Armani suits, to the diamond incrusted "Too Real For TV" pimp cup. He was well known, well respected, and good friends with Jackpot. They met last year at a Players Ball thrown by a west coast pimp name, Mack. Maroy hooked Jackpot up with a custom pimp cup, designed by "Debbie The Glass Lady" herself. Not that plastic bullshit you see in the back of the Source with the cheap rhinestones for $20. But the real deal $400 to $1,200 ones like Bishop Don Juan and LiL Jon had, which she also designed by the way.

One day, Jackpot was looking around trying to buy a cup before the Players Ball, not realizing who was the person responsible for designing them. He came across the fake ones, but he wasn't about to play himself with one of them. So he got ahold of Ka$hanova, a playa patna of his that knew Maroy, who informed him had the plug on the pimp cups.

Like Maroy, Debbie was from Chicago. She was also good friends with Maroy. Ka$hanova plugged Jackpot and Maroy a night before the Players Ball. Realizing that it would be too late for Jackpot to send the money and get the pimp cup designed before the Ball, Maroy took the money out of his own pocket, got it made, and told em he'd bring it to the Ball where he could pick it up and pay him there. All of knowing each other 5 minutes through a telephone conversation. That trust between the two cemented their bond and friendship in stone, and they've been fuckin with each other every since.

"Wuss up Playboy Maroy?"

"Nothing much P, just calling to see if you was gonna make it out to Pimp JuJu's Players Ball? It's to celebrate his birthday. It's suppose ta be real live jack."

"Is that right, where is it takin place?"

"In the Chi baby, where else? This suppose ta be the livest ball since the Bishop's."

"Sounds like the place to be."

"Hell yeah. All I gotta say is...don't meet me there, beat me there."

"Alright pimp suit well check this out, email me the info. But you already know, it's gonna be lights, camera, action with me baby. Shiiit, they might think it's my birthday." Jackpot said, as the two laughed, finished up their conversation, and hung up the phone.

After hanging up the phone and checking the time, Jackpot realized it was going on 9:00 p.m. He gave his hommie Phero a call and let him know that he wasn't gonna make it to DC because he had to get ready for the Players Ball next month which was only 3 weeks away. Instead, he was gonna send his hoes to Vegas and Reno, where he felt he could make more money with less invested. Phero said alright, and that he'd meet him in 3 weeks at the Players Ball as well. They chopped it up for about 2 more minutes and hung up the phone.

Jackpot realized, that he must have fallen asleep for a couple of hours from the blunt he smoked earlier when he looked at the time. Lisa and Yuki was still in their bedrooms as instructed, waiting for Jackpot to come talk to them about the fight they had gotten into. Jackpot was not in the mood. Knowing that both bitches was gonna point the finger at each other and not claim responsibility.

Jackpot had enough common sense to know without even talking to them that Lisa was more than likely the cause of the fight. Jackpot knew that

Lisa had been showing out a lot lately and acting real devilish. Yuki never got into it with any of the other girls, and none of the other girls ever got into it with Yuki. But, "all" of the girls got into it with Lisa on separate occasions more than once. Jackpot was beginning to feel like he may have to shake Lisa and let her go. He knew one bad apple spoils the bunch. He also knew that nothing's worst than the heart of a woman scorn, and with Lisa acting so devilish lately, he knew that if he fired or quit fuckin with her, it may cause even more problems. Jackpot knew that, sometimes you gotta make a bitch think she left you, just so she can feel like she got the upper hand and not get devious on you. Jackpot knew that wouldn't work with Lisa though because she'd been around too long and loved Jackpot to "death."

Jackpot walked upstairs and got Yuki's side of the story first, knowing that she'd be the most reasonable and easiest to deal with. Lisa's gonna be loud and dramatic to cover up the fact that she was wrong. So knowing this, Jackpot talked to Yuki 1st. Yuki explained to her folks exactly what happened and how everything went down from beginning to end. She explained how she just asked Lisa if she saw or had her purse, already knowing she did because Sunshine had already told Yuki she saw Lisa with her purse the night before. Yuki knowing how Lisa could be, didn't wanna get Sunshine involved.

So she asked Lisa the question like she didn't already know the answer, and that's when she snapped. Yuki explained how she feels like Lisa is jealous of her and don't know why because she's never did anything mean or foul towards her. Yuki told Jackpot that she doesn't trust Lisa and thinks that she's gonna do something scandalous one day and get them caught up. Jackpot felt the same way but knew he couldn't tell Yuki that, so he just assured her that he's very intelligent and well aware of everything that goes on around him. Even when it may look like he's not paying attention, he is. He told her, "sometimes you have to play a fool, to catch a fool. And though you may not understand what I mean by that now, later on you will."

Yuki knew what he meant. She was a lot smarter than he thought. Yuki had been with Jackpot for a long time and soaked up game like a sponge. When he talked, she listened. She didn't let his words go in one ear and out the other like most bitches do. And because of that, Yuki was like a female version of Jackpot. At that moment, Yuki knew that Lisa's days were numbered, and she wouldn't be around much longer.

Jackpot told Yuki, "no more fighting. The only person that's gonna be doing any hitting around here is me." Yuki shook her head and said okay with her head down looking like a little girl that just been scolded by her daddy. After Jackpot was done talking to Yuki about the fight, he let her know that she was going to Vegas for 3 weeks on automatic with her wifey's, with the exception of Lisa who was going to Reno to work at the Bunny Ranch.

Yuki smiled and got excited, almost forgetting about the fact she had just gotten chastised not even 2 minutes before. Yuki loved Vegas because, it was fast paced and she always made a lot of money. There's a pimp and hoe saying that goes... in Vegas, you're only 1 date away from retirement. Hoes is always on the hunt for that big lick. That million dollar trick. And some have found it. Like this one hoe that came across this one trick that had $500,000 cash in a duffle bag under his bed. He was stupid enough to show her. He was even more stupid to have fallen asleep. Needless to say, he woke up empty handed. And that bitch, nor his cash, have been seen or heard from since.

Jackpot told Yuki that he'd talk to her about Vegas a little more later, and that she could come out the room now. Jackpot left Yuki's room and went into Lisa's to talk to her next, where he knew the situation and conversation would be like night and day from the one he just had with Yuki.

"Alright, so what happened between you and Yuki?" Jackpot asked Lisa, as he walked in her room and closed the door.

"What, she ain't already tell you? All you gonna do is believe her and blame me like you always do."

"Bitch, who the fuck you think you talking to? I didn't come in here blaming shit! I asked you a simple fuckin question and all you had to do was answer the bitch. Hoe don't get besides yourself. I ain't one of these tricks or sucka for love ass niggas you be dating. You better respect the 'P' in my pimpin before you get and find yourself fucked up! Now lets try this again. What happened between you and Yuki?"

Lisa began to tell her side of the story, visibly upset but smart enough not to push her luck and piss Jackpot off any further. "I was in my room minding my business trying to get some rest, because I was tired from working real late the night before. Yuki comes into my room without knocking, waking me up talking about a purse or something. I was 1/2 sleep so I told her to leave me alone and get out of my room because I'm trying to rest. That's when she slammed my door and started talking shit about me to Green Eyes. Even with the door closed I could hear them talking. It made me mad cause I felt like they were gaining up on me like they always do." By now Lisa was in tears and acting emotional. Jackpot knew the ruse all too well and wasn't buying into it.

"Bitch you know the pimp doctor removed my heart a long time ago. So cut off the water works and finish telling the story. Them fuckin tears ain't buying you no sympathy." That's when Lisa got dramatic.

"I'm not looking for sympathy. I'm trying to tell you what happened and you're sitting there yelling at me."

"Bitch kill dat shit! Get to the fight and finish the rest of the story."

"Like I was trying to say...I heard Yuki talking shit about me. So I got out of bed, opened the door, and told her to keep my name out of her mouth. Then we started fighting."

"Who hit who first?"

"I don't remember."

"Oh now you don't remember, how convenient. Well let me ask you this, you saw Yuki's purse? Now before you answer, let me pre-warn you that if you lie and I find out, or if you say no and I find it in this room, I'm a kick your ass and have you touching everything up in this mutha fucka. You know I don't tolerate that lying shit. If you'll lie then you'll steal. That shit goes hand-n-hand, like a peanut butter and jelly sandwich with the crust cut off." Lisa thought about lying but knew that if her folks found the bag that was visibly hidden in her closet he was sure to kick her ass.

"Yes I have it. It's in my closet."

"So why didn't you just say that when Yuki asked you about it?"

"Because I was 1/2 sleep. Then once we started fighting, it was no longer about the purse. It was about her talking shit about me."

"Yeah always the victim right? Bitch gimme the damn purse. And the next time I hear about anyone up in here fighting over something so stupid, I'm a kick everyone involves ass. From this point on, none of ya'll take, use, borrow, or...'steal,' anyone else's shit without asking first. Break that rule, and I break a foot up in someone's ass." Lisa handed Jackpot the Gucci purse out of the closet. Jackpot then told her all about the Reno trip she was taking tomorrow and left the room.

15 $IN CITY

Sunshine, Yuki, and Green Eye's plane just touched down in Vegas. Lisa was on an earlier flight to Reno because the limo driver to the Bunny Ranch brothel was scheduled to pick her up from the airport at 12:00 p.m. From there she would go to medical and get screened and cleared for STD's. From there she would get cleared by the Sheriff department to work in one of Reno's legal brothels.

She usually worked at Sheri's Ranch because it was very clean, comfortable, and she always made a lot of money there. The Bunny Ranch was her 2nd favorite. This was the same brothel you saw on HBO and numerous talk shows. The only thing she "didn't" like about the Bunny Ranch was, the owner always wanted to fuck the girls. And the girls that didn't fuck him, usually didn't make any money. *Oh well, small price to pay to get paid,* Lisa would always say, "I've fucked for a lot less." Then she'd give him the time of his life and come back 3 weeks later $20,000 richer. Yuki, Sunshine, and Green Eyes got a limo, which is like getting a cab in Vegas, and took it to the Days Inn. Off the strip but not too far, that way it a still be easy, quick, and convenient to get to their calls. In Vegas, you work the casinos. That's where the money's at. Even if you're in a service, you still work the casinos.

The Venetian is where all the Pimps, Ballers, Hustlers, and Shot Callers like to go and gamble. This was also where very rich wealthy white men liked to spend money as well. Yuki and her wifey's knew this fact all too well from the numerous times they worked Vegas in the past. So with that being known...that's where the bitches headed.

------$$$$------

"Line up!" The bell rang and the Madam yelled out, as 2 prominent doctors stood before 12 of the most beautiful girls the Bunny Ranch had to offer, and Lisa was one of them. Lisa had a way of enticing the customers to wanna pick her over the other girls. She wasn't even the prettiest either, but she always got picked. While some girls would just stand there with the, "pleases don't pick me" look on their face. Or standing around thinking their looks was good enough to seal the deal and not smiling or making eye contact with the customers, Lisa was doing all of thee above, and then some.

Smiling, waving at the tricks with her 4 fingers in a fluttery motion, blowing kisses, batting her eyelashes, whatever it took. So as long as the line-up bell kept ringing, her pockets kept chinging. One of the doctors that walked in picked a young redhead girl with freckles for himself, and the other doctor chose Lisa. The other 10 girls that wasn't picked frowned, sucked teeth, and talked shit under their breaths as they rolled their eyes and headed back to their rooms in hopes that the next customers that came in, would pick them.

------$$$$------

"21, you win again Sir," the attractive female card dealer said as she flipped over the last card to reveal a Ace and a Jack. Jim Peterson was on a roll. Jim was a real-estate tycoon out of Atlanta. He made millions flipping properties and houses in the early 90's, then took advantage of the sudden wave and attraction to South Beach Florida by selling high end bay front condominiums before the market crashed.

Jim was now 44, single, and worth over $72 million. Yuki noticed the big stack of chips sitting in front of the gentleman at the high-rollers table. She knew that he had over a $100,000 in chips because of the colors that sat before him. The red chips was worth a $1,000 a piece, and she could clearly see over a hundred grand on the table, as well as a few black chips, which were worth $20,000.

Yuki noticed right away that the gentleman was betting a $1,000 a hand. She also noticed that he was caucasian, and one thing Yuki knew about caucasian men was...they loved asian women. So Yuki set her sights on the mark. Yuki strategically placed herself in eyesight at a bar across from the blackjack table where her target was sitting. As soon as him and her made eye contact, she smiled and gave him a flirtatious feminine wave. Yuki was a master at "fishing." This is what she liked to call it. She would always say, "you can reel in any fish, you just gotta have the right bait." Yuki watched the man excuse himself from the blackjack table, and make his way over towards her direction in the bar where she was sitting. "Hello, is this seat taken?" the gentleman asked, pointing to the stool that sat next to Yuki.

"It is now. Have a seat," Yuki responded.

"I couldn't help but notice you from over there while I was playing cards. Allow me to introduce myself if I may."

"You may." Yuki said, with a seductive smile. (*Bait!*)

"My name is Jim Peterson."

"Hello Jim, I'm Yuki. Delighted to make your acquaintance." Yuki stuck out her hand. Jim gently grabbed her hand and kissed the back like Billy D Williams did to Diana Ross in Lady Sings The Blues.

"May I buy you a drink?"

"You may," Yuki responded.

"So what are we drinking?" Jim asked, while signaling for the waiter.

"I'll have a Long Island Iced Tea."

"2 Long Island Iced Tea's please?" Mr Peterson ordered as the waiter went to go make their drinks. 15 minutes, and a half a drink later, Jim Peterson was cashing in his chips and headed upstairs to his hotel suite with Yuki.

------$$$$------

Sunshine took a limo to the MGM Grand upon finding out that Roy Jones Jr was boxing. She knew that major fight events drew in big crowds of celebrities, rich tricks, and the who's who in the entertainment world. When Sunshine arrived, the casino was packed. Rappers Snoop Dogg and Outkast was seen in the lobby. Ja' Rule and the Murder Inc camp was at the crap tables. Actor's Chris Tucker, Denzel Washington, and Jamie Foxx was in attendance, as well as a slew of others. Sunshine was dressed to kill in a Versace evening gown, Manolos, Gucci sunglasses, and a Faux Mink.

Sunshine worked the room like the professional whore she was. Catching the attention and lustful male gazed eyes, undressing her perfectly shaped frame as she walked by. Sunshine was trained to spot a rich man by the type of shoes he wore on his feet and watch on his wrist. So when she spotted the european man with the Presidential Rolex at the roulette table, she went in for the kill.

"Let me have $5,000 on red," the man said, as he placed his bet. At the same time he was placing his bet, Sunshine walked over and stood next to him.

"Black 28," the roulette attendant said, scooping up the lost chips as the ball nestled in the black slot of the round wheel slowly spinning in a circle.

"Now you know you're always suppose ta bet on black," Sunshine said to the man, in a very seductive and suggestive way.

"Is that so pretty lady?" the man said back.

"Alright then, give me a $1,000 on black."

"Make it twenty, because I have a feeling you're about to get lucky." Sunshine said, while biting the corner of her bottom lip. Just the mere site of such gave the man a woody in his pants. "Alright, I'm a gambling man, make it twenty." Sunshine crossed her fingers behind her back as she prayed the ball landed on black. The attendant spun the wheel and let the little white ball no bigger than the size of a large marble go. The ball went round and round in rotation a few good times before slowing down. when the wheel stopped, the ball did 3 more laps before parking into a slot and coming to a rest. "Black 22!" The attendant called out as she doubled the mans winnings. "See I told you, black was a 'sure' thing," Sunshine said to the man with that, "you can fuck me for the right price" look in her eyes. "Well from the looks of things, I guess it is," he responded back, grabbed his chips, stuck out his arm and said, "shall we?" Sunshine smiled took his arm and said with a lustful grin, "yes we shall."

------$$$$------

Green Eyes left the Venetian and went to Caesars Palace because way too many pimps kept trying to push up on her, and it was beginning to attract too much negative attention and effect her work. Green Eyes preferred Caesars Palace anyway because a lot of asians liked to go and gamble there and Green Eyes knew, asian men loved white women. Especially young white women. More or so, young "blonde" white women.

In Vegas, asians spend money like water. It's something in their genes. It's like they can't help it. Go to any casino, bingo or gambling reservation in America and look around. 70% of the players is asian. Another thing Green Eyes liked about asian men was, their boy size penis. This kept her shit tight and pussy from being overworked. The downside to the equation was, it made a lot of them prefer to fuck in the ass. Still being, Green Eyes didn't care, because that just meant double the price. As Green Eyes would say, "as long as you pay to play you can have it your way." She prided herself at being able to take it in both holes. When Green Eyes arrived at Caesars Palace, it wasn't even 5 minutes before she got the attention of a rich diplomat from China coming out of the casino about to get into a limo. As always, game recognize game and he knew right away that Green Eyes was a working girl the moment he laid eyes on her. The china man had his body guard approach Green Eyes with a proposition and offer she couldn't refuse. $2,500 to spend the rest of the evening with him. Green Eyes agreed, got into the limo, and they drove off into the night.

This was how top notch hoes got down. None of that crack whore, low bottom, $100 a date shit if you're lucky bullshit you got on Fremont Street. Those was the slums. Those was the hoes you saw on "Cops" getting arrested. Not even 10 minutes away from the strip next to the penny arcades and Greyhound bus station. Yeah that's right, "penny" arcades. Vegas wants all your money, down to the last red cent. This is the land where people lose their entire life savings in a card game. Is there really any wonder why there's a Pawn Shop on every corner?

------$$$$------

Lisa had a special request from the good old doctor and boy was she happy to oblige. He told her that he was straight and didn't consider himself gay but liked it when a female fucked him in the ass. *Yeah okay, not gay huh?* Lisa thought to herself, but was nothing she hadn't heard or been through before. Truth be told, there was a lot of guys out there getting down like old doc. Undercover brothers and homo thugs is what they called them. The type of men that would let another man suck they dick and not feel it was gay because they was on the receiving end. Or the husband or man that goes to prison and fucks a punk in the ass but says he's not gay because he was the one doing the fucking. Lisa liked it when she got these type of clients because she could take control and fuck the shit out of the trick like he would normally do her. She got great joy out of treating the man like a bitch, giving her pussy a rest, and making good money while doing so.

"Would you like a drink?"

"I'll have some champagne," Yuki responded to Jim Peterson. Yuki knew not to drink heavy or too much while on a date. So whenever she had to drink with a trick, she would usually request champagne and sip it. Jim poured Yuki a glass of expensive champagne after corking the bottle and letting it breathe. Yuki knew how to relax her clients, so after their drinks, she set the mood by giving Jim a sensual back rub and massage. "You like that?"

"Oh yeah, that feels good baby." Jim responded, on his stomach laying across the king size bed as Yuki kneaded his back like dough in a pizza parlor. Her hands was like magic. Even her folks would tell her so from time to time. By this time, Jim was turned on hot and ready to fuck. "So, how much for full service?"

"$1,000 for an hour and I promise, it'll be a night you'll never forget," Yuki whispered in his ear, sitting on his back while he was still lying on his front.

"That's all? Well, I'll double that, plus give you an extra $1,000 if you can make it a G.F.E (Girlfriend Experience)."

"Make it 5 and you have a deal. And I'll throw in a dinner with that considering you've been nothing but a gentleman so far." Yuki wasn't really into the GFE, because it was a lot more personal. It involved kissing, hugging, sometimes talking, and possible dinner or more. Basically, you was ones girlfriend for the night. Yuki hated having to be intimate with a trick in a way that she usually saved for her folks. But for $5,000...shittt, a bitch just gonna have ta do what she gotta do.

"Okay, deal," Jim said, as he pealed off fifty $100 bills from the chips he cashed in earlier, gave em to Yuki, and started their date.

------$$$$------

"May I eat your pussy?"

"Yes, but it's gonna cost you extra," Sunshine said, smiling with her pearly whites brightening up the room like the sun. Sunshine had a fat pussy that for some reason, tricks always wanted to eat when they saw it. As much as she hated them licking on her, for the right price, they could. Sunshine didn't like the fact of a tricks saliva being all up in her pussy and between her legs. She hated any type of body fluids that wasn't hers on her body. So where as most hoes would have been like, "fuck yeah you can eat my pussy," Sunshine was like, "Hell No!" Unless your money was longer than your tongue, it wasn't going down. "Well darling, as I'm sure you can see, money ain't a thing. Just name your price." The european trick responded, with a slight accent pouring himself a drink from the fully stocked bar in his hotel suite. The trick noticed Sunshines pussy and the fact that she didn't have any panties on when they first arrived back to his suite and she sat down and crossed her legs, 1 over the other like Shannon Stone in Basic Instincts.

"Well how about we negotiate one flat rate big spender? Sayyy...$4,000 for everything?"

"Everything?"

"Everything!" Sunshine said, licking her top lip while opening and crossing her leg back over to the other side revealing yet again that fat pussy of hers. The trick said, "done. I would have given you 5."

"That's fine, because I would have taken 3." He laughed and said, "I like you." Jim finished up his drink, taking it down in one swig, placed the glass on the counter, took $4,000 worth of chips off the dresser, handed them to Sunshine, and started their date.

------$$$$------

Green Eyes knew that by the end of this date she would be walking out with a lot more than $2,500. That was just to get in the car, but he didn't know that. She knew right away from the diplomatic plates on the limo that Mr Lee had money. She just didn't wanna overplay her hand when they first met. But she knew, once she got in his head...and not the head on his shoulders either, he would give her anything her pretty Green Eyes desired. "So what's your pleasure sweetie?" Green Eyes said to Mr Lee, flashing her Green Eyes sitting on the long side of the seat in the stretched limo. Lee was a small little man with a big and powerful presence. One of his bodyguards sat across from Green Eyes in the limo, the other sat in the front seat next to the driver.

"Me horny for american girl. Looking for good time while in merica," Mr Lee said, with a strong asian accent.

"How much fun you looking to have?" Green Eyes asked.

"Enough sucky to last long time. I pay good. Money no object."

"Glad ta hear and see we're on the same page."

"You stay night to morning I pay eight thousand dol-la." *Shiiit, that's a no brainer*, Green Eyes thought to herself but still managed to play it cool. "Deal, and for that I'll be sure to make it a night to remember and one you'll never forget." For the rest of the night Green Eyes accompanied Mr Lee as his official arm candy while he gambled the night away calling her his good luck charm.

By 5:00 a.m. they called it quits and headed back to his private suite on the top floor of Caesars Palace. Before walking inside, Green Eyes said, "You know I never did get your name. All this time we spent together tonight and neither one of us thought to ask or tell." The asian diplomat laughed and said, "You can call me Mr Lee."

"Happy to meet you Mr Lee, and you can call me Green Eyes." For some reason, Green Eyes didn't believe that Mr Lee was his real name, but really could care less as long as she got paid her money.

Mr Lee had already payed her the initial $2,500 to spend the night being his escort and exotic arm candy. He promised her the other $5,500 once they got back to his suite at the end of the night. when they walked into the suite, the place looked like a royal palace. Gold fixtures, jacuzzi tub in the living room, California king size bed, roman pillars, statues, and a fully stocked bar. The place was stacked. Green Eyes walked inside and made herself comfortable while Lee instructed his bodyguards to stand outside. When Lee came back inside the suite he handed Green Eyes the rest of her money and told her, he had a fetish of being beat and humiliated and would like her to partake in that with him. Green Eyes didn't have a problem with it as long as she was gonna be the one doing the humiliating. To her, that was easy money.

Mr Lee told her that he was gonna go inside the other room and change into something more comfortable. 10 minutes later Mr Lee came out in some fishnet stockings, garter belt and red pumps with a baby diaper on. He looked ridiculous. It took everything in Green Eyes power to keep from laughing. "I've been a bad boy and need spanking," Mr Lee said, in a whiny baby voice with an asian accent. Green Eyes played along.

"Crawl your ass over here and lick my heels!"

"Yes mistress." Mr Lee got on all fours like a dog, crawled over, and licked Green Eye's Gucci pumps. Then she smacked the shit out of his ass and said, "take it off and suck my toes you piece of shit." Mr Lee took off her shoe and did as instructed. While sucking on her toes in between licks, Mr Lee started making baby noises and pointed to a sex whip and leather paddle that was sitting in the far corner on a table. Green Eyes mushed him down with her foot, walked over to the table, and grabbed the paddle. From there she went back over to Mr Lee, spun him around and spanked the shit out of him. The shit turned him on so much that he got an erection. Then the scene got weird and down right disgusting. Green Eyes noticed a foul odor when Mr Lee said, "baby go boo boo."

"Oh hell nah! No this mutha fucka didn't," Green Eyes said to herself at the thought of a grown man in a child's diaper shitting on himself. That just pissed her off more. Green Eyes went over to the table and grabbed the whip. "Take this you nasty chinky eye bastard!"

"Yes mommy pun-ish me." Green Eyes swung the whip and smacked him across the face like Indiana Jones. That turned him on more as he moaned and pissed himself. Green Eyes couldn't believe the shit she was seeing. She had thought she saw it all, but this trick was something else.

For the next 45 minutes she beat, spit, kicked, whipped and humiliated Mr Lee into an orgasm. When it was over he turned back into Mr Lee the chinese diplomat, not Mr Lee the pervert. Lee went back in the other room, cleaned up, and put his regular clothes back on. Lee thanked Green Eyes for a wonderful night and escorted her to the door. Green Eyes left the hotel suite never to see Mr Lee again. She couldn't help but think to herself, *shit, if people only knew.* But this was Sin City. Vegas. And what happens in Vegas...stays in Vegas.

16 THE INTERNATIONAL PLAYERS BALL

It had been 3 weeks since Jackpot's hoes went to Vegas. And now they were back home and over $50,000 richer. This boosted up the hoes morale 10 folds. Money can fix a hoes attitude and put a bitch in check like the ink on a payroll slip. At least for the time being. Everybody was happy and getting along with each other. For a while it felt like old times. Jackpot's plan worked out to a "T."

Absence makes the heart grow fonder, and Jackpot knew he had to have his bitches in a positive state of mind and at their best for the Players Ball. The first night the hoes came back, everything was all good and like old times. They had a 5-way freak session that wore Jackpot out. The next morning everyone went shopping for the up and coming Players Ball. Jackpot had already had his suit custom made from the foot up. A one of a kind. One he would only wear once. Just for this special occasion. The suit was all gold with actual 24k gold trim throughout. The buttons was pure 2k white diamonds, with no flaws. When the lights hit those diamonds, it looked like mini disco balls. JP was embroidered on the jacket pocket with 24k gold thread. He had gold money bag cufflinks flooded with diamonds and his initials to bring it out. He had a custom $1,200 tie with his initials throughout as well, identical to the design on his cufflinks, made from the finest italian silk that money could buy. He had a matching handkerchief made from the same silk for his jacket pocket, with a money bag tie clip to match his cufflinks. All-in-all, his suit was worth more than $70,000. No joke. And mind you...he only wore it once.

------$$$$------

First stop Jackpot made was to Price Breakers in National City off Plaza Blvd. This place was like a mini Fam-Mart but the jewelry was a lot better. This was where Jackpot got his custom pieces from. Although their jewelry store was located in San Diego, their high end pieces was created and shipped from L.A. Jackpot had just got a custom 3 finger ring made of him in a pimp stance standing up surrounded by his 4 hoes who were at his feet.

The ring stood 4 inches off his fingers looking like a small statue. All gold of course flooded with diamonds. The shit was worth $60 grand easy, but he got it for forty. "Damn! that shit is on deck like a Carnival cruise ship or pack of cards in Vegas. Ooh wee, look at them diamonds," Jackpot said with excitement as the jeweler showed him his newly created custom ring. "Now that's what I'm talking bout there jack. Shit, pimpin finna show out." As if that wasn't enough. "I threw in a little something extra, since you spend so much money with me," the jeweler said. "What's that?"

"Check it out." The jeweler placed the ring on Jackpot's fingers and said, "alright, pay attention to the girls. Now flick your hand down." The hoes head's were on some type of swivel device. So when Jackpot flicked his hand, the hoes head's looked down towards the ground. "Oh shit, get the fuck outta here!"

"Yeah, I knew you'd like it." Shit, Jackpot more than liked it. He loved it. He loved it so much that he gave the jeweler an extra $1,000 tip. "They don't call me Jack The Jeweler for nothing," the jeweler said, smiling while giving Jackpot dap.

"Alright G, well I gotta head out. I got my bitches in the car waiting and I'm sure by now they're getting restless like a bunch of kids waiting in line to ride a roller coaster at Six Flags." JP broke Jack off $41,000, told him again, "good looking out" on the ring and left the shop. Now Jackpot was set. He didn't need to buy any shoes because his gator collection would put a zoo in Florida to shame. He had a pair to match any and every outfit, with more color combinations than 31 Flavors.

Jackpot was ready to take Pimp of the Year at JuJu's Players Ball. On Bishop Don Magic Juan's birthday, the biggest Players Ball event of the year, Jackpot took the trophy for, "Most up and Coming Pimp of the Year," for how quick he came up in the game. Now Jackpot was ready to be recognized as the pound for pound hands down Pimp of the Year. He met the full criteria. His money was long, game strong. House right, cars tight. Stable in pocket and diamonds bright. Even Jackpot's hoes was flossing with cars, clothes, and jewelry that could put an average Chili Pimp to shame. His bitches fur game was mean. Minks in every style and color. His hoes kept dead animals on their back. And their jewelry game was on point as well. Every one of Jackpot's hoes had a custom name plate that said, "UNKNOCKABLE," with princess cut diamonds and a small elegant chain worth $10,000 a piece.

This was how you kept a hoe down and around. While other pimps kept their bitches broke and looking average, Jackpot kept his hoes broke and living lavish. A hoe would have to be stupid to leave this situation. What grass was greener? Not to mention, Jackpot was still getting by with beating a bitch with words, rarely ever having to result to putting hands on a hoe.

Jackpot took his hoes to Saks & Neiman Marcus to get them something for the Ball. Whatever they decided on had to match. At least to a certain degree. Where as, even if they stood apart, you would still know by their outfits that they were together. Jackpot got off on the Hotel Circle freeway exit and headed to the mall that housed Seau's Place. A sports bar built and owned by the ex San Diego Charger Jr Seau. Jackpot usually let his hoes shop for themselves, but with this being such a special event, he wanted to supervise and make sure they picked outfits that would compliment each other, as well as his suit.

"Alright, ya'll know the deal. I want ya'll to pick out the flyest shit ya'll can find. I wanna see ass, tits, and hips. Think on the lines of LiL Kim on the red carpet at the Music Awards. Get whatever ya'll want. But make sure it matches with one another. It doesn't have to be the same outfit...shit, it a probably be better if it wasn't. But it does have to look like we're a family and came together. So whether that's material, same color or pattern scheme, etc. Just make sure it match." With that being said, the hoes agreed and went to find their eye popping, jaw dropping, award winning outfits for the Ball. A fit to wear standing behind their folks as he excepts the trophy for Pimp of the Year.

That is, if he was lucky and fortunate enough to do so. And truth be told, luck had nothing to do with it. It was all about how much work you put in the game. The more you put in, the more you got back out. Period! That's the formula. You gotta be Internationally known, locally excepted, and truly respected. Cross Country Pimpin! That's how you get recognized. And there's no short cuts to that jack.

------$$$$------

"Hi, I'm Galaxy Glen. Your host with the most on the red carpet of this years International Players Ball. This is already turning out to be a start studded event. Playa's from all across the country have turned out to celebrate Pimp JuJu's birthday and show out. We got a limo pulling up now." A long super stretched Benz limo pulled up to the red carpet. The driver got out and opened up the rear door and let out a pimp and 3 hoes. The bitches had their heads down and never looked up once. The pimp wore a blue and white 2-toned suit with blue and white gators. His hoes had on blue and white matching Prada dresses." Hey hey pimp, welcome to the 2000 International Players Ball and JuJu's Birthday Bash." Glen greeted the pimp.

"Thank ya thank ya, glad ta be here."

"You looking real sharp too."

"Yeah yeah, you know pimpin had ta show up and show out."

"Right right. So who do you think is gonna take Pimp of the Year tonight?"

"Shiiit, me, who else?"

"Okay okay, well there it is. We'll be looking for you pimp." Galaxy Glen shook his hand as the pimp and 3 hoes walked inside the Ball.

"We have another limo pulling up. This is your raving pimp reporter Galaxy Glen bringing it to ya." The doors opened and out stepped a light skin pimp with a red and white pin stripe suit, red gators, full length white mink with a matching fur hat. He had 2 bad ass white hoes with him that didn't look a day over 20.

"Kenny Red just stepped in the building folks." Cameras flashed and videos rolled as Galaxy Glen spoke. "What it do pimp?"

"Oh you know I had ta ride all the way cross country and let em know that K-Red ain't dead and that's all that needs ta be said. I've been grinding like a meat factory and plan on taking one of them there trophies home tonight you dig?"

"Yeah I can dig it, I can dig it. Well good luck to ya pimp." Next, an old school Rose Royce pulled up. A white guy dressed like a pimp stepped out in a Versace suit and mink coat with matching gators and handed the valet his car keys.

"As you can see, we have none other than White Folks in the house. The only white pimp I know hated by a few but respected by all. Wuss up playa?"

"Ah you know, just tryna get chose out in this piece. Hoe blew up on pimpin last week but still ain't gonna stop me from flexing my mouth piece. You know wut I'm talkin bout?"

"I got you pimp. Well you know it ain't nothing but fresh meat inside. And, you're looking sharper than a knife in a penitentiary fight..."

"So all pimpin gotta do is stay on his tools while spitting these jewels and everything should go smooth," White Folks cut him off and finished.

White Folks had game. If you were to close your eyes and listen to him talk you would have sworn that it was a black man speaking to you. White Folks walked inside as Jackpot's limo pulled up. The driver got out and opened the back door. Jackpot stepped out suited and booted as cameras flashed and jaws dropped.

Yuki stepped out next and placed a mink cape with the initials "JP" on the back and placed it over Jackpot's shoulders. Green Eyes stepped out next, holding a custom pimp cane with..."Let Me Pimp Or Let Me Die" going down the side in diamonds. She handed the cane to Jackpot and stood to his left. Lisa stepped out of the limo next with a large Pimp cup in tow. Big enough to hold an entire bottle of champagne. It was gold plated with "Jackpot" flowing around the top in diamonds.

The cup was already filled to the brim with Cristal. Lisa handed Jackpot the cup and stood to his right. Sunshine stepped out last, holding a big chain and medallion as well as the new custom ring Jackpot had just got made of him and his 4 hoes. Sunshine placed the chain over Jackpot's head and the large 3 finger ring on his fingers and stepped to the left. The hoes all wore matching Gucci outfits from head to toe and chocolate colored minks. "Damnnn playa! Call the coroner cause you tryna knock em dead tonight," Galaxy Glen said, greeting

Jackpot, talking into the mike. "Oh yeah you know mayne, nigga tryna get that Pimp of the Year. But what they need ta go on and do you know, is gimme that Mack of the Decade cause I'm killin em in a real way. Who you know doing it like me on theez streets?"

"Right right, I hear ya playa. Shit, well ain't no secret your name been ringing..." Jackpot cut him off.

"Look here pimp. It's gonna be a close race for 2nd place, but 1st is gonna be a land slide like 3rd base or home plate, ya dig?"

"I can dig it, I can dig it. Well shit, you might come up on more than a trophy tonight looking like that jack."

"What you think the limo's for? I'm tryna double up like a D–Boy, snatching hoes from them decoys, while keeping this izm, space age like Elroy, you understand me? You don't hear me tho."

"Well I'm too near ya not ta hear ya pimpin."

"Alright pimp suit, well let me go on and walk inside so they know that your royal heinous, Daygo's finest has arrived. Jackpot took a sip of Cristal from his pimp cup and walked inside. Inside was packed with over 300 of the most famous pimps in the world. Jackpot went to the V.I.P section and sat down. The front of the stage was lined up with trophies. Famous rapper Ice–T was hosting the event.

On the stage, there was a box with a small slit cut on the top. This was how pimps payed there respects and celebrated another pimps birthday, with cold hard cash! Pimps was placing $50/$100 bills in the box through the small slit all night. Some would show out and put more, you know to floss, like money ain't a thang. Even with that,

Jackpot couldn't be faded. Jackpot walked over to the stage and said, "pimps up to my hommie JuJu. Happy birthday pimp!" and placed a $1,000 in the box. Too Real For TV was in the building filming as usual. Maroy approached Jackpot, with his video camera crew and mic in hand. "Wuss up pimp?" Maroy said to his pimp patna Jackpot as they gave each other a pimp shake and playa Greeting. "Pimps up hommie, wuss good wit cha?" Jackpot answered back.

"Nothing much, just the same old, same old. I'm bout ta put out a new DVD. Cross Country Pimping, remember I told you about it?"

"Oh yeah at the last Ball. I remember you talking bout it."

"So you know the DVD ain't gonna be official if I don't get my man Jackpot on it."

"Fa'sho. Roll camera pimp." Jackpot said then snapped his fingers. All 4 of his hoes stood up on cue and stood behind him. Maroy signaled his cameraman to roll film and looked into the camera. "This is Playboy Maroy from TooRealForTv.Com. Nickel slick and a hoes first round draft pick. At the 2000 International Players Ball and JuJu's Birthday Bash. As you know, Too Real For TV is always in the place and in your face. We here tonight with Jackpot Tha Pimp. A well known and well respected pimp out of San Diego. This is one of the coldest macks ta ever do it at a young age. Wuss up pimp?"

"Pimps up wit'cha!"

"So I hear you're in the running for Pimp of the Year. How does it feel to be nominated at a young age, going up against some of the coldest and oldest pimps to ever live?"

"Well you know, it ain't the age but the stage. I stayed down for my crown and put it down for my town. I played the game big and got big results. I feel I earned this title. I've touched every major track in the country. Pimped and served more news than CNN. I got the finest hoes and flyest clothes. Game tight and money right with a million dollar appetite."

"Okay, I feel you pimp. I see you done stepped up a few pieces as well since the last time I saw you," Maroy said, pointing at Jackpots new and well crafted 3 finger ring.

"Well you know this a little something to always keep the pimpin in perspective ya dig? Dis here is me and my 4 main bitches. As you can see they're outta pocket, as you gaze into their diamond incrusted eye sockets. But with a flick of the wrist, the hoes bow down." Jackpot flicked his wrist, and the hoes heads dropped to face the floor, at the same exact time, perfectly in sync with one another, the actual hoes standing behind Jackpot did the same.

"Now if that wasn't pimpin then I don't know what is," Maroy responded, flabbergasted by the sight of what he just witnessed. Maroy asked a few more questions and finished up the interview. Jackpot gave him a pound and made his rounds throughout the Ball. In the back, Pimps was taking pictures in front of a big airbrushed backdrop that said, "Players Ball," with a Cadillac drawn in the middle. "Jackpot!"

JP heard someone call his name from the photo booth area but couldn't make out the face through the bright lights. As he got closer he saw a pimp in a 2 tone blue and white suit with 3 bitches with their heads down. Right away JP knew who it was. "Snooky my man!" Jackpot said, greeting him with a one arm hug and a handshake. Snooky was a cold die hard pimp out of Milwaukee. His bitches had to keep their heads down looking at the ground at, "all" times. He gave a new meaning to the phrase, "staying in pocket." He would say, "a hoe a tell you what a nigga's 'gators' look like...but not what his 'face' look like." Snooky won Pimp of the Year the previous year at Pimpin Ken's Ball. "Take a picture wit a pimp!"

"No doubt," Jackpot responded. the 2 went in front of the airbrushed backdrop and flicked it up. The photographer told them to come back in 10 minutes to pick up their pics. "Yeah you know I'm coming for that title pimp." Jackpot said, semi joking but very serious. "We'll see about that jack."

"Yeah that trophy you won last year was so big they said, all the buildings in New York could fall and that trophy a still be standing tall." The 2 laughed as Snooky co-signed the fact. "You betta believe it. It took 2 of my hoes just to carry the mutha fucka."

"Well as you can see, this years competition is fierce, but pimpin ain't pimped until they met a pimp like me. Please believe it." Jackpot and Snooky kept chopping it up and high signing about who was gonna take what trophies home, how many hoes was gonna choose up and get knocked before the night was through, and shit like that.

Snoop Dogg and chairman of the board for Famous Players Bishop Don "Magic" Juan, stepped in the building. Snoop had on a red wine color leather coat with white mink fur throughout it. The same coat he wore in the movie Boss'n Up. Don Juan was in his signature colors, green and gold. For those that don't know, green is for the money and gold is for the honey. Bishop had on a green mink coat with gold mink buttons. He had a green and gold mink hat to match. His suit was tailor fit and custom made. It was money green with dollar signs all over it and glitter throughout, to catch the lights. Of course he had on matching green and gold gators to set it off. He had a long custom made cane, also known as a "Pimp Stick," with, "Bishop Don Juan" running down the side. A pimp cup with, "Magic Juan" in diamonds along the side as well. An old school rope chain with a cross large enough to put some rappers jewelry to shame. And last but not least, his "Magic Juan" 4 finger rings flooded with diamonds on each hand.

In this environment, Snoop Dogg wasn't the celebrity, the Bishop was. He was Snoop Dogg's ghetto pass to the underworld of Pimps-n-Hoes. While Snoop Dogg was rapping about the game, most of these cats was living it.

Good Game was standing across the room in a carmel colored mink and matching brim. When he noticed Jackpot, he raised his pimp cup and nodded his head like, "wuss up?" Jackpot return the gesture as he walked back to his table, sat down, and enjoyed the nights entertainment. JuJu had Suga Free come out and perform for his birthday. The show was live, and everyone enjoyed the performance. Jackpot noticed something to his left that made him do a double take. It was a female surrounded by 6 hoes. At first he thought it might have been just 7 hoes sitting together. But upon further inspection, he noticed that the one in the middle was dressed like a pimp. He couldn't believe his eyes. Never, in all his few years of pimpin has he ever saw, or came across a female pimp. Shit, in his mind and world, that just didn't exist. Not to mention, the bitches were carrying on like a bunch of lesbians instead of a pimp and her hoes. They was sitting around kissing and grinding on the bitch. *What the fuck part of the game is this?* Jackpot thought to himself, as he sat back and watched in amazement. "That's a damn shame. How's pussy gonna pay pussy?" Lisa said, as Green Eyes, Yuki, and Sunshine laughed in agreement.

"I know that's right," Green Eyes said, slapping Lisa a small high five like 2 fans at a football game. Guess they weren't the only ones who felt like that, because no sooner than Lisa made the comment, $upreme, another pimp out of Daygo that owned his own escort service and record label, was all over the bitches. He was spitting his pimpin and blasting at the hoes. Saying they needed to come home to some real pimpin and quit hiding up under that pussy. Pimpin had to have balls to play this game, and he didn't see any balls on her. $upreme was going at the hoes hard, but they stood their ground and by their bitch.

Jackpot just laughed, sat back, and ordered a bottle of Cristal for his hoes. Jackpot couldn't help but think how ridiculous it would be to get knocked for one of his bitches by another bitch. Just the thought of such a thing made Jackpot laugh again, but this time to himself. The waiter returned with the hoe's bottle of Champagne. The waiter corked the bottle and poured them each a glass, then set the bottle back down in a bucket of ice and placed it on the table. Jackpot gave the waiter $350 plus a $50 tip. The waiter thanked him and left as Jackpot and the girls toasted the night away.

Outside on the red carpet, Fuk-A-Bitch was making a late appearance. F.A.B was another pimp that came a long way throughout the years. In 98, the tracks in Cali was getting slow and he had burned too many bridges in the East Coast from being so cut throat. So F.A.B took a trip to ATL and came up. The hoes were fast but the game was slow, and F.A.B took advantage of the fact. In Atlanta, nigga's go to strip clubs like the rest of the world go to regular clubs.

F.A.B's first night in Atlanta he discovered Magic City. A small hole in the wall strip club located downtown, down the street from the Greyhound bus station that attracted the cities most prominent D-Boys and Hustlers. The bitches here was nothing like hoes in Cali. In Atlanta, even the white girls got ass. This place was like the strip club capital of the world, and bitches was getting money. This wasn't like California. Nigga's here, loved to trick. Their motto is, "It ain't tricking if you got it," and these boys had it. In Cali, tricks was putting dollars in hoes G-strings. In Atlanta, they was throwing it in the air. And we ain't talking about no mutha fuckin ones either. We talking two, three, $400 thrown in the air at a time like nothing. D-Boys blowing $15,000 to $20,000 a night like its water.

F.A.B couldn't believe his eyes. From then on he started working the strip clubs as well as the track, and hasn't looked back since. He put Katt up in Magic City, and his other bitch worked Fulton and Industrial. The pimps had a good program and nice little set up the way they worked the blade on Industrial. What they would do is, rent a bunch of rooms at the Travel Lodge. The pimps would stay in one room, and their hoes would work out of the anothers. Instead of drawing a bunch of attention by posting up and working the streets, they would post up behind the hotel, way in the back where police or vice couldn't ride up on them without being seen. If police did come through, the hoes would just scatter like roaches back to their rooms before being spotted. Once gone, it was back to business as usual. This little method made it quick and easy for hoes to pull dates, as well as, pimps keeping an eye out on their hoes from the shadows of their hotel rooms. With so many hoes in Atlanta use to fucking with black tricks, it took no time for F.A.B to trick and gorilla hoes outta pocket. ATL wasn't ready for that Oakland game or mentality and F.A.B took full advantage of it. Now he was 8 deep with no sleep and ready to take, "Pimp of the Year."

"We got a late arrival. But you know, as they say, better late then never. What it do pimp?" Galaxy Glen said, pointing the mic in F.A.B's direction to get his reaction

"Well you can already tell, by the ice in my grill and them 16 stiletto heels, that it's pimpin wit me jack." F.A.B responded.

"Well I see you're looking good and hotter than a hooker in Arizona."

"Yadada mean? I came ta snatch up that Pimp of the Year."

"Well let me tell you, competition is tough."

"So is dis game jack, yadada mean?"

"Well good luck ta ya."

"Thank you pimp. But you don't need luck, when you got game, 8 hoes, and a stack like mines." F.A.B finished talking and walked inside. When F.A.B walked inside the Ball, the trophy ceremony was already taking place. Good Game had won for Cross Country Pimping. He won that award for being recognized coast to coast on every track in America. To win that award, you had to really be putting in some major track time like a locomotive or San Francisco trolley. Snooky won for the flyest

Jewelry. Jackpot felt like he should have won that one for his ring if nothing else. But he knew and understood that when the nominations came down and a winner was chosen, his ring was still in the shop getting made. So no one knew about his new ring until today, which was actually too late.

Next time, that trophy's mine, Jackpot thought to himself. Don Juan was hosting the award ceremony and handing out the trophies. "This next award goes to...Jackpot! for best dressed. Come up here and get your trophy playa."

Jackpot stood up, raised his pimp cup, then walked on stage to get his trophy. Once on top of the stage, he did a half circle and stood in a Superman pose with his cape shinning. His hoes stood up and cheered him on while bowing their head and hands like a peasant to their king. Most Active Player went to $upreme. He was recognized for being the first pimp to own his own escort service and rap label. He was well known, well respected, and only 22 years old.

His brother Ka$hanova, won Most Improved Player for how quick he came up and got back on his feet after doing 6 years in the penitentiary for a pimp charge he caught in Vegas. Phero won the Smooth Player Award. The ceremony went on for a good 45 minutes. White Folks won The Lifetime Achievement award and got a standing ovation. Probably because, he was a white man playing a black mans game, and playing it to the fullest. You couldn't do nothing but respect that. All-in-all, it was a good night. Over 20 to 30 pimps and macks had received various awards acknowledging their achievements within the game. Now it was time for the big one. The moment that everyone was waiting for. The award and trophy that meant the most. The reason so many pimps showed up in their best threads, jewelry, and hoes. Pimp JuJu did the honors of announcing the candidates and winner for International 2000 Pimp of the Year.

"Okay everyone. Pimps, macks, and hoes of all ages. This is the moment we've all been waiting for." JuJu spoke into the mic. "This year we have 3 nominees for Pimp of the Year and let me tell you that the judging was close. Picking a winner was no easy task. Let's first start off by thanking the judging panel, chairman of the board and directors of Famous Players. Now without further or do, I'd like to bring to the stage our first nominee. Kenny Red! Come on down playa. Our second nomination goes out to a real cold die hard pimp. If you've been in the game long enough, I'm pretty sure he done knocked you for a bitch or 2."

The crowd started laughing. "Fuk-A-Bitch, come to the stage playa!" F.A.B walked on stage with his stable of 8 bitches. As he stood on stage, all of his hoes kissed his gators and bowed down in a half circle around him. When Jackpot saw F.A.B and the big medallion around his neck with the initials "F.A.B," his mind instantly flashed back to 4 years ago in Oakland sitting at the stoplight next to a cat in a red Mustang with the "F.A.B" license plates. Then he thought about the allege incident that took place between Green Eyes and a pimp name Fuk-A-Bitch. That's when he put the 2 names and face together. He always heard of Fuk-A-Bitch and all his gorilla tactics throughout the states, but he never physically ran into him again after that one day in Oakland at the light. "And last but not least, our 3rd nominee. Jackpot!" JP smiled and headed towards the stage with his 4 hoes following close behind. Fuk–A–Bitch looked just as shocked to see Jackpot as Jackpot was to see him when they announced F.A.B as the 2nd nominee. F.A.B had been hearing through the pimpvine that Jackpot was doing big things. Jackpot's name was ringing on the streets. Even though F.A.B had 8 hoes, only 3 of them was top notch, and 5 of them was black. Jackpot's hoes was all bad bitches and top dollar money makers. Jackpot knew that 4 bad bitches beat out 8 average hoes any day. Still, never the less and with that being said, Jackpot knew that he'd be lying to himself if he didn't admit that he was still a little nervous.

"And this years 3rd runner up is...Kenny Red!" JuJu announced, and the crowd cheered. "And now for our International 2000 Pimp of the Year. Jackpot!" Jackpot put his head down and fist in the air. The crowd clapped and cheered. "Pimp Pimp, hooray! Pimp Pimp, hooray!" the crowd chanted as Jackpot stepped to the mic to make his acceptance speech.

"It's been a long road to get here, and a pleasure to be amongst so many die hard, 100%, cross country pimps like myself."

"Preach!" a voice said from the crowd. "This one's for all the pimps that keeps a foot in a hoe's ass and mash for his cash. From a hoe's cock into a pimp's sock. I'd like to thank the board, Don Juan, JuJu, and every pimp and hoe cross country nation wide. Pimps up, hoes down. Chuuuch!" The crowd stood up and chanted. "Pimp Pimp...Hooray! Pimp Pimp...Hooray!" JuJu handed Jackpot the 6 foot trophy. Jackpot grabbed it by the sides with 2 hands and put it in the air high above his head. This was the best day of Jackpot's pimpin life. Since the 1st day a hoe checked a dollar and placed it in his hands. A pimp will forget about many of the hoes he had in a lifetime, but never the 1st. This day felt like the first day Yuki broke luck. Jackpot was excited and would never forget it. Jackpot handed the trophy off to Yuki and Green Eyes as they stood on either side holding it up. Jackpot walked off the stage with his hoes not too far behind, while F.A.B mean mugged and envied the fact of Jackpot taking 1st place and him only getting 2nd.

From that moment, F.A.B vowed and made it his business to knock one of his hoes, if not the whole stable, when and if he ever got the chance. Before it was business, but now it was personal. What can you say, even some pimps have the hater bug within them. Once bitten, you're a hater for life. How else can you feel comfortable gorilla pimpin the next man for his hoe instead of finessing your own. With all the mouth piece and game in the world, you'd rather kidnap a bitch, throw her in the trunk, and make her hoe for you? Terrible! And that's why cats like F.A.B in the game don't last long.

17 THE BEGINNING OF THE END

2 Years Later

Things had been heating up and getting bad for Jackpot. Lisa was officially out of control. She stopped getting along with her wife-n-laws all together. Now, all they did was fight. Lisa was 28 and damn near pushing 30. Once a bitch hit 30 she was passed her hoe prime. In the game, that was considered old.

Even though Lisa still looked good and not a day over 25, her age still bothered her. She was very self conscious and envious of the other girls about it. Although she would never admit it, this was the main reason behind her jealousy. Lisa was like 2 people in 1 body. Sometimes she could be cool as ice and sweet as candy, and other times she could be down right devilish. Detective Spyder and Brittle had been getting closer to busting Jackpot. They came across 2 hoes that use to belong to Jackpot that were willing to testify against him. This was the detectives big break. They hadn't been able to pin anything on Jackpot in over 2 years because he'd stop shitting in his own backyard and worked exclusively out of state. This was good and bad because, now if he got caught or arrested for Pimping he could face White Slavery charges, which meant that he took a hoe across state lines with the intention to pimp. Not only are those charges a lot more serious and carries a lot more time, but they're also federal, and would put him in the federal Penitentiary.

Jackpot was beginning to feel like the walls was closing in on him. He could feel the heat coming down on him. He always felt like he was being watched or followed. Sometimes he would see weird stuff like, police rolling down his block real slow and then just stop in front of his house and wave. They weren't even trying to be sneaky or hide the fact that they were watching him anymore. Shit was getting tense. And to make matters worst, Lisa managed to run Sunshine off. She was too fragile and couldn't deal with her shit anymore.

One day Jackpot came home from The Blue Tattoo, a local club in the Gaslamp District in downtown San Diego. When he walked into Sunshine's room to check in on her, the room was empty and all of her stuff was gone, with the exception of the note on the dresser that said...

Dear Daddy,

Sorry I had to leave this way but things just aren't the same. As much as I love you, I no longer love this situation. Lisa is the devil and she cannot be trusted. I really don't think you realize what she's capable of, but I do. I see the look in her eyes and the way she treats me and the other girls when you're not around. I no longer feel safe and I really can't take it anymore. When we said it'll be "Till Game Do Us Part" I truly felt that, and now it's game over =(I'm sorry Daddy. Take care

Love,
Sunshine

------$$$$------

That was a year ago, and things have been going downhill every since. One day, Jackpot was at the A.V.N Awards and Porn Convention in Vegas when he saw Sunshine and 2 white girls standing together by one of the porn booths. When he tried to approach her, she put her head down, went the other way and stood behind what obviously had to be her pimp. When Jackpot got a good look at the fella with the gold teeth and slim build, he realized it was Fuk-A-Bitch.

Jackpot's stomach sunk like the Titanic, even though he didn't show it. If the pimp doctor hadn't removed his heart a long time ago, at that moment, it would had been broken. F.A.B just gave Jackpot a look like, "I told you I'd snatch one of your hoes," with a sly and devilish grin, shaking his head up and down. Jackpot just kept it pimpin as best he could, raised his pimp cup to F.A.B, and walked away. Jackpot always blamed Lisa for losing Sunshine and running her off, which only made the tension grow stronger between them. Now she wasn't just tripping with the girls, but with Jackpot as well. The bitch was too comfortable and acting out every chance she got. Due to all the constant drama, morale was down. Which meant, money was down, and Jackpot wasn't nearly stacking and putting away as much as he use to.

His bitches was starting to get lazy. Green Eyes was starting to lose respect for Jackpot for not getting rid of Lisa a long time ago. You know the saying, "1 bad apple spoils the bunch," and they ain't never lied. Lisa was rotten alright. Rotten to the fuckin core, and it took Jackpot entirely too long to realize it. This was a sinking ship going down fast. Money began to get so slow that Jackpot had to dig up and go into his stash a few times just to stay afloat.

The tracks was slow and the services was flooded. Unlike when he 1st had started fuckin with em. You'd be lucky to find 5 girls working for any giving service, and most never worked pass 2 a.m. Now, every pimp on this side of the border had his hoe in the service, and Jackpot's pockets felt it tremendously. Yeah he was still making big money, but he also had big expenses and high bills.

People don't understand how the rich get poor and file for bankruptcy. It's because, when you make millions you spend millions and once you spend millions you have to, "maintain" millions. Period! That's how Donald Trump owns a billion dollar casino and high rise hotels and still file for bankruptcy 3 times. So with all the bullshit Jackpot was going through in the game, his pockets was taking the hit. Jackpot would always tell himself, "as long as my bills are paid and I got hoes on the blade...I'm straight!" But he also knew that living day to day with no food put away was a dangerous game to play. Shit was coming down harder than a brick from the empire state building. The game was like a roller coaster. Many ups and downs, but it was the twist and turns that caught you slipping. And now everything was coming to a head. Life as Jackpot knew it was about to take a turn for the worst.

------$$$$------

"**Bitch, get your lazy ass up!**" Jackpot hollered at Lisa who was still in her bed sleeping.

"Shit! what the fuck's wrong with you? Lisa responded. That set Jackpot off like a pit-bull in a dog fight.

"Hoe, who the fuck you think you talking to?" Jackpot yanked Lisa up by her neck and slapped the shit out of her. Lisa screamed like a chick in a horror flick. "Bitch, shut the fuck up! Why you ain't out getting my money hoe? It's fuckin ten o'clock and yo ass sleep. You think you got it like that bitch?" Jackpot smacked her again. Now Lisa was crying, tears running down her face like a faucet. Jackpot grabbed her by the hair and drugged her across the room like a caveman. "Bitch, you got me and the game fucked up! You been getting way too loose wit the lip lately. Hoe, you think you running shit? Only person running shit here is me. I'm the Captain of this mutha fuckin ship bitch." Jackpot kicked the hoe in her back. "Daddy, why you doing this to me?"

"Bitch, you did it to ya'self. You wanna run round here fighting muh fucka's, well fight me hoe!" Jackpot had so much pent up anger that he couldn't stop himself. He knew he was going too far, but oh well. The bitch deserved it. It's been a long time coming and Jackpot had had enough. If you let a pot over boil, shits gonna evaporate, and that's how Jackpot felt about his stable. Shit had been boiling up to this point for a long time. And do to the fact, his money's been evaporating, as well as his hoes for that matter.

Jackpot prided himself in being the type of pimp that was able to pimp with his tongue and not his fist. Yeah he smacked a bitch around from time to time, but nothing like this. Jackpot knew that Lisa was to blame for a lot of the hardship that he was going through. What made him angrier was when he kept it real with himself and knew that it was actually, "His" fault. He was to blame, for not pimpin harder and pimpin smarter. He should have gotten rid of Lisa a long time ago at the first sign of deceit. But instead, he kept her around. All for the greed of the mighty dollar. Going against his own beliefs which is, "all money ain't good money," and, "sometimes what's good to ya, ain't good for ya."

Now Jackpot had finally had enough but it was probably too late. Lisa was a very vindictive female. She felt like Jackpot owed her the world for sticking by him so long and holding him down. As much as she loved him, she would see Jackpot dead before seeing him happy with someone else and not her. "Bitch, get your ass dressed and the fuck out my house, you're fired!" Those last 2 words echoed in Lisa's head like a bullhorn.

"After all I did for you, all the money I made, you just gonna throw me out and get rid of me like a piece of trash?"

"No, not like a piece of trash. Like a piece of shit! Now get your fuckin clothes on and get out before I change my mind and throw you out butt necked."

"Okay, after all I've done. Alright." Lisa had a look on her face that could give Charlie Manson the creeps. Lisa hurried up and got dressed and left, but not before saying..."this ain't the last you'll hear from me!" and slammed the door.

------$$$$------

Boom!!!

The front door gets kicked in at 5:00 a.m. "Get the fuck down! Police, everybody get down on the ground and don't move!" Jackpot was awakened by the sound of the San Diego P.D., Sheriffs, Vice and Special Unit Squad. He was taken completely by surprise and off guard. Jackpot was cuffed and brung downstairs to find Yuki and Green Eyes cuffed as well, sitting on the living room couch. As Jackpot got to the bottom of the stairs, Detective Brittle was standing there with a shit grin and said, "I knew we'd get your black ass."

"Fuck you, you fat hating burrito eating mexican piece of shit!" Jackpot responded, which wiped the shit grin off the detectives face like a box of Cleenex. "We'll see how much shit you're talking, when you're somebody's bitch in Folsom. Take em downtown to central booking boys. Take the whores to Las Colinas." Brittle instructed his men, as him and Detective Spyder surveyed the house.

"Look at this shit, fucking nigger was living like a king. All my years on the force and I couldn't afford a house half this size. Stupid bitches. Why would you pay a low life piece of shit nigger money for selling your pussy all night, just to make him rich?" Detective Spyder said to himself, but loud enough to be heard by his partner.

"Beats me. I've been trying to figure that shit out for years," Brittle responded, while look, and feeling on the Versace print curtains covering the windows in Jackpot's room. The cops ransacked the house, looking for large sums of cash and expensive jewelry that they could confiscate and book as evidence. They took pictures of the house and its contents. The fancy furs, and exotic cars in the garage. 2 days later, they came back with a warrant to seize everything inside. They took 5 cars including the 2 that Sunshine and Lisa left behind.

Although most hoes would have taken the car when they left, Sunshine didn't wanna leave scandalous, nor have to go about life looking over her shoulder. Not only that, but she felt bad enough for leaving Jackpot the way she did in the 1st place. She truly did love him. But in the game, love had nothing to do with it. And in her heart, she knew this day would come. She was cashing in her chips while she was ahead. That would prove to be the smartest move she ever made. The dumbest, was getting with F.A.B afterwards.

Lisa, never got a chance to take her car with her which only left her more bitter. So now the police was confiscating a total of 5 cars, all luxury automobiles. They found Jackpots stash in a small safe in the closet. He had $50,000 cash, but with no legitimate job to prove where it came from, they were able to confiscate that too. Only $40,000 showed up to evidence, go figure. All of Jackpot and the girls jewelry was seized as well. They took all the pimp trophies Jackpot had won throughout the years as evidence too, along with his custom hand crafted pimp cups and pictures of him with other pimps and hoes at the Players Ball.

They had a lot on Jackpot, but nothing was worst and more damaging than the 2 alleged hoes the police had that was willing to testify. And now to add fuel to the fire, they recently came across a 3rd informant willing to testify that could really send Jackpot up shits creek with no paddle. The pigs had Jackpot by the balls, and that night, they celebrated and toasted the fact, at a small bar in Pacific Beach where local cops like to frequent.

18 PENITENTIARY BOUND

Jackpot was booked on 5 counts of Pimping and Pandering. If convicted on all counts, he could face 30 years in the penitentiary. Yuki and Green Eyes was booked for prostitution. Their charges were only misdemeanors and not that serious. If convicted, they only faced 6 months to a year. Jackpot called his bail bondsman and got them out right away.

Jackpot wasn't as lucky. His bail was $500,000 and because of the nature of the crime, the prosecutor and judge said that JP had to prove where every dollar came from, down to the red cent if he posted bail. He couldn't put up his house as collateral because the cops seized it. The only other route Jackpot could think of was his mother, and in his book, that wasn't an option. He wasn't about to burden her with a misfortune that he brung on himself. So for the next 6 months while Jackpot fought his case, that's where he sat. In the San Diego County Jail. Almost all the money that Jackpot had was gone with the exception of the bail money and the $20,000 he had stashed on the side of his mothers house for a lawyer. Jackpot thanked the heavens that he was smart enough to put some money away for a lawyer. You don't know how many hustlers was doing it big on the streets, then got arrested and couldn't even afford a lawyer because he foolishly spent his money on cars and jewelry, none of which is gonna get your black ass out of jail once you get arrested. Now they're on their way to getting fuckin railroaded by a public pretender.

Jackpot called his momma and told her the deal about his case. Then he let her know where his money was buried at and instructed her to dig it up and retain a lawyer. Jackpot was housed downtown for 3 days then transferred to George Bailey Detention Facility. In Bailey, the jail politics was high. Mexicans didn't fuck with the blacks but fucked with the whites. Whites fucked with the mexicans but not the blacks. And the blacks didn't fuck with neither one of them.

Even the indians ran with the whites, which made no fucking sense to Jackpot. He looked at the indians like a bunch of house niggas that didn't know their history. The white man took their land and wiped out whole tribes. Now here they was, riding with them. *Backwards mutha fucka's.* Any race other than black, white, or mexican, fell in the category of "other" and ran with the blacks. So needless to say, the black car was short. But what the blacks lacked in numbers, they made up for in power. Bailey was nicknamed, "The Thunder Dome," because of its frequent race riots and fights. The mexicans were broken up into 2 groups. The Pisas, and the Serenos. Serenos ran up under the Mexican Mafia umbrella. There was no such thing as a 1-on-1 fight with a mexican. If you got into it with "1," then you got into it with them all. The whites fell into a few categories as well. A regular white boy was considered a Peckerwood or, "Wood" for short. Then their was the Skin Heads and Nazi Lowriders. Those were the racists mutha fuckas. The blacks was either, Blood, Crip, or non affiliates. A lot of inmates that was scared or didn't wanna fall up under the jail politics ran with the "Christian" car. A lot of inmates found God once they came to jail. Some were sincere, but most was full of shit. Upon their release from incarceration, they'd hit the streets and commit the same crimes that got them locked up in the first place. *Fuckin hypocrites,* Jackpot thought to himself, when he saw them in their prayer circles clutching their bibles and preaching to others. Jail was no place for a pimp. Jackpot felt like a caged animal in a zoo for the wild.

------$$$$------

Jackpot had been arraigned today and his readiness hearing was set for 4 weeks from today. He had waived his bail review when his lawyer told him, it'd be a waste of time due to the number of charges he had. If they couldn't get his bail under $10,000, which they couldn't, then he'd be in the same boat of having to provide proof of employment or where he got the money from to bail out. Not only that, but, the $20,000 that he paid to retain him only covered everything up until trial. If they couldn't get the charges dropped or a sweet deal from the D.A. then they were going to trial, which would cost an additional $20,000. So it was wiser to hold on to the bail money just incase he needed to use it for trial. Jackpot agreed. As bad as Jackpot wanted to get out of jail, he knew the smart thing to do was to, stay in and stick it out. So he did just that. Yuki and Green Eyes did what they did best and hit the blade to get up some scratch. Yuki moved back in with her friend in East Daygo, and Green Eyes moved in with one of her sugar daddies.

At first, Green Eyes and Yuki would visit Jackpot every weekend, nothing less than 2 times a week. But as time went on, the visits from Green Eyes started to slow down. Yuki kept it strong and always made sure Jackpot had money on his books. She made sure he always maxed out at commissary and always excepted his collect calls. It was 3 days before Jackpot's readiness. He was laying on his bunk chopping it up with his celly, when a voice came over the intercom…*"Walters."*

"Yeah."

"You got a visit," the C.O. informed over the loud speaker. Jackpot got up and threw on his state blues, checked his appearance in the make shift mirror above the sink in his 5x9 inch cell, and went to his visit. Jackpot loved his visits, but he hated the process you had to go through beforehand. The deputies always made you strip down to your underwear, before and after every visit. This shit didn't make any sense to JP considering that the visits were behind glass. Nevertheless, this was the rule.

"Walters," the deputy in charge of taking the inmates up to their visits called out, standing in front of the cell door that separates the housing unit from the sally port. "Yeah, I'm here."

"Last 4?"

"5,5,0,0." The cell door opened up after confirming that the numbers matched the inmates. Once a person's locked up, their no longer a person but a number. Your number identifies who you are. Jackpot stepped into the sally port, went through the usual drop your pants dance, and walked upstairs to his visit. When Jackpot walked inside of the visiting room, Yuki was already there, sitting on the other side of the glass patiently waiting for her folks. Jackpot sat down in front of her, smiled, and picked up the phone. "Hey Baby how you doing?"

"Alright I guess," Yuki responded.

"So you know I go to court in 3 days right?"

"Yeah I know, I've been calling everyday keeping up with you."

"How's work?"

"Slow, I got a few stacks put away."

"A few stacks, how much?"

"Like three"

"three! that's it? Shit, you use to make that in one night."

"I know Daddy, but it's hard out here by myself. I'm use to you taking care of me and all our finances. I have to help pay the rent where I'm staying at, since the police took my car, I've been having to pay for a rental. The blade is hot, the service is slow. I don't know Daddy it's just hard."

"I know Babe, but life is hard and only the strong will survive. You've been with me a long time and I taught you almost everything I know. You gotta think like me. You have to maneuver and make wise decisions. You're my bottom bitch." Jackpot never called her that before. He didn't believe in it. He didn't like the thought of giving 1 bitch special attention and placing a hoe up on a pedestal above the rest. The wrong bitch could let some shit like that go to her head, and the end result wind up being more harmful than good. So he always told his hoes that they were equal and that no one was bottom. But once in jail, a mutha fucka gotta say and do what ever he has to, ta keep a bitch down and around.

"You hear me Babygirl?" Yuki's eyes lit up like christmas lights from Jackpot's last statement, and he knew it too. It was written all over her face how good, and happy it made her feel.

"Yeah, I hear you Daddy."

"So you have to think and move like a bottom. You're not new to this, so hoe hard and stay true to this."

"I will Daddy, it's just been hard without you."

"I understand. A hoe without guidance is like a turkey with his head cut off...it's gonna run around the yard bumping into everything until eventually, it keel over and die. Where's your wifey at?"

"I don't know Daddy. I haven't talked to her in a week."

"What, is that right? Jackpot responded, semi shocked, but had a good feeling Green Eyes might be falling off due to the lack of visits he was receiving from her. Every now and then he would get a letter from her talking about she's still down, till game do em part and blah blah blah, but most of the time it just came across as a guilt letter.

"Last time I talked to her Daddy, she said she was going up to Vegas to work. When I offered to go with her, she shun me off. Then she said, she had to go and would get with me later. Needless to say, that was monday and I haven't heard from her since."

"Damn, is dat right? Okay, don't trip. Just focus on what you need to do, I'll deal with Green Eyes. For now, I need you to get that bankroll up and stack them chips for when I get out. My lawyer said 2 of the charges should get dropped monday because you and Green Eyes aren't testifying against me. But the problem is, they still have 3 bitches that is."

"That's fucked up Daddy. Who do you think it is?"

"Shit, who knows. Could be anyone. Probably one of them old Choosey Susie bitches I done had in the past."

"You think Lisa might be one of the girls?" The very thought of Yuki's question sent chills through Jackpot's body. It wasn't like he hadn't thought the same thing from time to time himself, while late night thinking sitting on his bunk. It was just the fact that he knew, unlike most of the hoes he knocked, that chosed up then was gone after a couple of weeks or months was...Lisa knew enough of his business, and been around long enough to really take him under. She was the smoking gun. As much as Jackpot tried to dismiss the thought. Deep down, he knew that it was a very real possibility. Rule #1...trust no bitch. Rule #2...**TRUST NO BITCH!**

"I don't know Babygirl. Anything's possible. But I would hate to think so." With that being said, the phones shut off signifying that visiting time was over. Yuki blew Jackpot a kiss as he went back to his dorm.

"Okay, the D.A. is offering 12 years if you plead today. She's willing to drop 2 of the charges and have you plead out to 3. The charges carry 2, 4, and 6. So she's willing to give you the mid-term." Jackpot's lawyer spoke to JP in the courts bullpen explaining the deal the D.A. was throwing on the table. "Now I'm not gonna shit you. They have 3 pretty credible witnesses according to the D.A. All girls who've claimed to be with, and work for you at some time or another. Now with that being said, I still feel like this isn't much of a deal and the D.A. can do better."

"I agree," said Jackpot. "I never even been locked up before. Jail, nor the penitentiary. So I don't see why she would give me the mid-term instead of the low term and run everything concurrent."

"You're pretty smart for someone who's never been locked up before. Maybe you should have been a lawyer," the lawyer said jokingly. But Jackpot wasn't laughing. "Well it's because, this particular D.A. has it in for you. She hates pimp cases and takes them very personal. That wasn't a surprise to Jackpot. Shit, what bitch had love for a pimp other than a hoe? He knew he was up against it.

"Did you find out who the girls testifying is?" Jackpot asked.

"Yeah, a girl name Nicky and Tony. The 3rd girl is a surprise witness that the D.A.'s keeping under wraps until the pre-lim." Jackpot remembered the bitches vaguely. Nicky was a hoe that made a mad move back in 98. She left her chili pimp because she felt like he wasn't giving her enough attention. When she thought the grass was greener on the other side by choosing up with Jackpot. She quickly realized that it wasn't when she couldn't compete with his other hoes. With her ex-pimp, she felt like a big fish. But in Jackpots stable, she felt like a guppy. The hoe didn't even last a week before she was back with her old pimp. Jackpot wasn't too worried about her because he knew that she didn't know enough about him. She wasn't around long enough. That would just come down to her word against his.

Tony was a hoe Jackpot had in 2001. He had her longer than Nicky, but never brung her to his house, or introduced her to the rest of his stable. For good reason too. He never trusted her, and knew she was the jealous type that like to come through a pimps stable like a hurricane, and run off everything in sight. But she was a hella money maker, so Jackpot fucked with her at a distance. He got a good run out of her for about a month before she blew up and chose a pimp name Goldie. This too would be a case of Jackpot's word against hers.

But what about this surprise, "star" witness? That might be a different story. If the D.A. was keeping her a secret, it had to be for a reason. Jackpot rejected the D.A.'s deal and his lawyer set a date for the preliminary hearing.

Yuki and Jackpot's mom and sister was in the courtroom for support, but Green Eyes was not present. The bailiff escorted Jackpot back to the bullpen, then moments later, out the courtroom. Jackpot's preliminary was set for 60 days from the day so that his lawyer would have enough time to prepare his case and go through all of the discovery. The gray goose (prison bus) took Jackpot back to Bailey and to his cell where he spent the remainder of his day, on his bunk, and in his mind. Thinking of what was yet to come... **PRISON!**

"All rise." Green Eyes had all but fell off by this point. Word on the streets was that she had started smoking crystal, and Jackpot believed it too. All the signs were there. The last time she came to visit JP she was about 20 pounds under weight and had visibly picked her face so bad, that it looked like she had an extreme case of chicken pox. She looked tore up. And to make matters worst, she had tweeker jaw. This was when a persons bottom jaw was twisted like they had a stroke. The bitch looked nothing like her former self.

When Jackpot walked into the visiting room he hardly recognized her. He asked her if she was using drugs, but of course she denied it. Jackpot wasn't no fool though, and he knew better. That was a month ago. That was also the last time he saw or heard from her. Yuki was still holding it down. She wasn't making money like she was when Jackpot was out, but she was maintaining and staying afloat.

Today was the big day. The pre-lim. Today the judge would rule if there was enough evidence to go to trial or not. This was also where the D.A. would have to unveil their star witness. Yuki and Jackpot's mother was positioned in back of the court to the left, low-key sitting behind Jackpot. From time to time, Jackpot would turn around in his seat where he was shackled sitting next to his lawyer, and smile at his mother, sister and Yuki. Yuki blew him a kiss, and his mother would throw him a, "keep your head up" smile. This was when the bailiff told everyone to rise, announced the judge, and brung the courtroom to order. The prosecutor submitted their case to the state and got the proceedings on the way. The pre-lim was like a mini trial without a jury. The judge would listen to all the evidence submitted and witness testimony, then decide if it was enough to go to trial. The prosecutor painted Jackpot out to be a monster. A predator that prayed on women. Jackpot thought to himself, *bitch, you're only 1/2 right. I am a predator. One that prays on "hoes," not women.* But he didn't dare say that out loud.

The D.A. put Nicky and Tony up on the stand and made them look like victims. They came into court looking squarer than a box of crayons. They had on their sundays best. Jackpot thought, *man these bitches don't even dress like that. You hoes is putting it on thick. Where's the fishnet stockings and high heels ya'll had on when I met ya'll?* Jackpot couldn't help but think what he do to a bitch so bad that she had to go through such extreme measures to cross him up? He always played the game fair.

He was taught, "Be good to the game, and the game will be good to you." But now Jackpot was finding out that, that wasn't always true. What did he do to these 2 hoes that would make them go against the grain, sing like a canary, and start snitching? He never even laid hands on these hoes. He was beginning to feel like maybe he should've. At least then they'd have a reason to be running their fuckin mouths.

After the 2 hoes was done giving their testimony about how they came to know the allege pimp that sat before them. Jackpot's lawyer crossed examined them both, finished up, and then the judge excused them from the stand. That's when the prosecution called their star witness to the stand. "The state would like to call Lisa Mae to the stand." A cold chill went through Jackpot's body, like a butt necked eskimo in a igloo, as he slowly turned around in his seat to see Lisa, his ex-hoe walking through the courtroom doors approaching to take the stand.

Jackpot knew he was toast like bread on the breakfast table. As Lisa walked pass Jackpot to take the stand, she turned and gave him a look like, "I told you I'd see you again." When Jackpot looked into her eyes all he saw was Satan. *How could this be the same bitch that I was with, and took care of for so many years?* Jackpot thought to himself. The saying was true, "Hell has no wrath like the heart of a woman scorned."

"Do you promise to tell the truth, the whole truth, and nothing but the truth, so help you god?" the bailiff asked as Lisa had her right hand up and her left hand on the bible.

"I do," Lisa responded and sat down at the judges request. The prosecutor asked, "Do you know a person by the name of Ricky Walters, also known as Jackpot, or JP for short?"

"Yes."

"Can you please point him out if you see him in this courtroom today?" Lisa looked directly at Jackpot and pointed to him. For the first time in Jackpots life, he was hurt behind the actions of a woman. From that very moment, everything went downhill. Lisa spilled it all. She helped connect every dot that the prosecution already had a clear picture of. Her 22 minute and 30 second testimony sunk Jackpot quicker than the Titanic. She told it all. From how they met, to how they split up, and everything in between. Jackpot's lawyer did his best during cross examination to paint a picture of a disgruntle ex-girlfriend that was lying and saying these things about Jackpot because he had broke up and ended the relationship with her, but was not successful. The judge wasn't buying it. He bounded the case over for trial 3 months from the day, banged his gavel, and that was that. Jackpot's goose was cooked like a christmas duck.

------$$$$------

Jackpot sat in the dayroom with a O.G. Blood from Lincoln Park turned player name "Money," playing chess. Jackpot passed most of his time playing chess. He loved the game. This was how he kept his mind clear and sucka free. Money was in his late 40's and down on a parol violation. He was waiting to be transfered any day to Donovan State Penitentiary. It sat right across the road from Bailey. Jackpot and Money would play chess everyday and chop it up about the game. "Yeah slick, I should be on my way to Donovan any day now," Money said, while pushing his white pawn to the black square.

"Yeah, I thought they was gonna roll you up last night." Jackpot responded, pushing pawn as well. "Me too. Well when I leave, make sure you continue to stay sucka free. Jail is for haters, gang bangers, and pimpatraters, all willing to do you harm."

"Yeah, I can dig it."

"Don't just dig it, but live it. Look here young blood, let me pull your coat to something." Money slid his rook in front of Jackpot's king and checked him. "Never get comfortable or careless in a place like this. Because as you know, even a king can be, **CHECKED!** I've been doing this a long time and one thing I learned is, what you practice here, is what you'll take to the streets. Use this time to sharpen your game." Jackpot moved out of check and Money continued talking. "Never put anything pass a bitch." Money moved his queen in front of Jackpot's king and checked him again. Especially when you already know what she's capable of...**CHECKMATE!**" Money lined up his queen with the rook and bishop and mated Jackpot's king. Jackpot always took Money's wisdom to heart, as well as his chess game. Chess is the game of life, and this is why he loved it so much. If you're gonna pimp, then you have to stay three steps ahead of the game like chess. Work that bitch to protect her king. Never underestimate the pawn game because a pawn can come back and hurt you. A nigga might be a pawn today, and a knight tomorrow.

Jackpot had thought he mastered the game, just like he thought he mastered chess. Until he learned, even the best player can get checkmated. After playing chess with Money, Jackpot grabbed the newspaper, and went into his cell to read. *Nothing interesting or out of the ordinary.* Jackpot thought, until he came across an article that caught his eye. The headline read, **"Pimp kills Prostitute In A Deadly Rage."** Jackpot read the story...

Okaland California

Jamal Jackson, a known Pimp from California was arrested last night for murder in the first degree. Witnesses say that they heard arguing between a man and a woman coming from a near by apartment followed by a loud scream and gun shots. Police arrived shortly after to find one dead female, and a male suspect covered in blood. The blood was believed to be the victims. The male was taken into custody without incident. The name of the victim has not been released because family had yet to be notified.

Jackpot didn't recognize the name, "Jamal Jackson," and wondered who he was. He also wondered how the police knew that the woman murdered was a prostitute. "Probably some fake ass chili pimpin nigga with one hoe and in love with the bitch, couldn't stand seeing her leave him and killed her. Shit, just something else to give the game a black eye," Jackpot said to himself. Jackpot folded up the newspaper, put it on the floor, laid across the bed, and fell asleep, thinking about the game.

------$$$$------

"Chow time!" Jackpot awoke to the sound of his cell door opening, and the inmate workers serving breakfast. **"Last call, bottom tier!"** The food server made his final announcement. Jackpot got up and washed the cold out his eyes then headed for the dayroom where chow was being served. Jackpot hated morning chow, because it was at 4 in the morning. When most pimps & whores was finishing up their nights and going to sleep, he was waking up to eat. This was something that Jackpot would never get use to. Jackpot grabbed his hot and cold tray and sat down on the black side of the module, at a back table in a section where all the blacks sat down to eat. That's when he noticed the tension. One thing about jail and prison is, when there's tension, it's usually so thick you could cut it with a razor blade. And that's when it happened.

A black man started arguing with a mexican worker over his food tray. Jackpot couldn't make out what was being spoken, but body language said it all. The black inmate punched the mexican in the face, knocking him out before he even touched the ground. All the mexicans in the dorm stood up and rushed the blacks like a swarm of killer bees protecting their hive. Jackpot hurled his food tray like a frisbee and caught a mexican in the neck. From there, he just started swinging for the fences, dropping any mexican within punching range.

The mexicans had the blacks outnumbered 3 to 1. And it didn't help matters that a few of them so called wannabe hard ass gang banging black mutha fucka's ran straight in their cells and locked it up when the riot kicked off. Yeah they wasn't talking that Blood, Crip, and Gangsta shit now. *Fuckin busta's!* All the mexicans got down. Even the old ones. That shit's mandatory with them. Jackpot ended up finding himself surrounded by 3 mexicans with sharp pencils in their hands as weapons. Money grabbed one from the back and put him in a bone crushing bear hug, before slamming him to the ground, damn near snapping his neck. This caught the other 2 mexicans off guard and Jackpot reacted accordingly. Money was getting old, but still had that penitentiary size that a man gets only from doing time. So even while pushing 50, he was "NO" slouch. Jackpot kicked the shit out of the other mexican and made him drop the pencil. The 3rd one caught Jackpot slipping and stabbed him on the side. Jackpot's adrenalin was so pumped up that he didn't even feel it. Nigga's and essay's was fighting, sticking, and dropping like flies. The jail alarm was going off but no one payed it any mind.

5 minutes into the melee, the goon squad rushed in shooting bean bags and tear gas all blacked up in riot gear with electric shields, trying to bring order and peace to the module. Jackpot covered his face with his county blue shirt and ran in his cell for cover. Jackpot wasn't no punk when it came to fighting and getting down, but bean bag guns and tear gas was the deal breaker. Getting shocked or hit with a wooden block was where Jackpot drew the line. Chess 101, know when the game is over.

It didn't take long for the goon squad to gain order. For the next 72 hours, the whole module was on lockdown. Some inmates got transferred and some went to the hole. Jackpot went to medical, got his side stitched up, and was sent back to the dorm. Many was injured, but no one was killed.

------$$$$------

"Mail call!" the deputy sounded off as he began to pass out mail. "Walters, last 4?"

"5,5,0,0," Jackpot responded. The deputy handed him and envelope. It had been 2 months since the riot that took place between the blacks and mexicans. Since then, the module had flipped. A lot of people either got released or sent to the penitentiary. Some got transferred to other facilities and a few was still there fighting their cases or doing county time. Drama was down and tension was low, at least for now. Jackpot looked at the front of the envelope to see who sent the letter. He was shocked when he read the name in the top left hand corner.

"Green Eyes." Jackpot said to himself, shocker than a husband walking in on his wife having sex with the local mailman. Jackpot hadn't heard from Green Eyes since the last time she came to see him all smoked out. Jackpot took a look at the return address and noticed that it was from Las Colinas Detention Facility.

"Oh this bitch done got herself arrested and now she wanna holla at pimpin huh?" Jackpot said to himself frowning, face twisted up so tight it revealed his right dimple. Jackpot sat on his bottom bunk and took the letter out of its envelope. He got up and took a bag of tea out of his commissary drawer and made himself a hot cup. Jackpot put the remainder of the tea in the bag away, closed his commissary drawer, sat back down on the bed, and read his letter.

Dear Daddy,   9-16-02

        Let me start by saying, I'm sorry it's been so long since you've heard from me. The last time I saw you I was so ashamed when you noticed and asked me if I was on drugs. After that, I didn't know how to face you. Life was so hard for me out here on these streets without you that I turned to drugs to numb the pain. Then before you knew it, I was hooked.

    You always told me that a hoe needs guidance. At the time I thought that was just some Pimp game you was running on me. But now I know it's true. =(As you can see, I got myself caught up in a bad situation and now I might be facing some real time. I got caught in a stolen car that I didn't know was stolen with this trick and a half ounce of crystal. The stolen car charge I can beat because I wasn't driving, but the dope they found on me.

    Well you always told me that Karma's a bitch, and what goes around comes back around. I don't expect you to forgive me Daddy. I know I messed up. I know I let you down when you needed me the most. And for that, I wanna say that I'm truly sorry. I still love you and "nothing," will ever change that.

                                    Love,
                                    Green Eyes

Jackpot finished the letter with mixed feelings. The pimp in him said, *"fuck that bitch she left me for the dead."* But the lonely male inmate side of him, felt sorry for her and tried to rationalize the situation. Either way, he wrote back.

Green Eyes,   *9-19-02*

Wuss up Babygirl? Sorry to hear about your dilemma. Even though I was very upset about how things turned out, I would never wish jail on you. I always told you that you got what you put out in life. So if you put out shit, then you're gonna get back shit in return. You can't do bad and think that good things are gonna happen for you. Life just doesn't work like that. But I'm not gonna kick a person when they're down so we'll just leave it like that.

I know it took a lot of guts for you to write and I appreciate it. You know we've been through a lot together so, I can forgive you but, I'll "never" forget. It's funny how people take life for granted until someone snatches their freedom away and then they realize what they had all along. But sometimes, by then it's too late and things can never be the same or go back to the way it was. Good luck with your case, and I wish you the best.

                                 Forever Mackin,
                                     Jackpot

Jackpot knew that when things started going bad for a bitch, the first thing she thinks about is how good life was before they started fucking up. Even in the square world. The minute a mutha fucka realize the grass is not greener on the other side, they wanna hop back over the fence. Only a sucker would allow this, and Jackpot was no sucker. Now with that being said, Jackpot also was no fool. He knew that it was a great possibility he might be doing some time, and what good is a pimp to a hoe in jail?

So instead of running the bitch off completely, he knew that it was a lot smarter to stroke the bitch ego, put her on the back burner, and play a fool to catch a fool when the time was right. He knew that by him writing back, as long as she was locked up she'd keep in touch. Now when she get out might be a different story. But fuck it! He'll worry about that then. So Jackpot addressed the letter and put it in the outgoing mailbox, went back to his cell, and went to sleep.

For the next couple of weeks, they wrote back and fourth and kept in touch. For a moment, it even began to feel like they might be able to put the past behind them and concentrate on the future. This is called, "jail writing." That's when a person's locked up, and they tend to say all the right things. Then they get out and all that shit they was talking goes down the sewer with the toilet water. That's why you never believe what a mutha fucka tells you when they're locked up. A person locked up a tell you they're gonna put your broke horse in the Kentucky Derby, only to have made "dog food" out of his ass when they came home. So after 3 weeks, Green Eyes went to court and got her charges dropped down to a lesser charge. The judge sentenced her to an outpatient program and time serve. Now it was back to...out of site, out of mind. Once Green Eyes got back on the streets, she stop writing Jackpot. 1 week after that, she was back on the dope...terrible!

------$$$$------

"Walters, you have a pro visit come to the gate." The deputy's voice blared over the loud speaker. Jackpot put his county blues on and walked to the gate. "Last four?" the deputy asked.

"5,5,0,0." The steel bar gate slid open as Jackpot answered and walked through. When Jackpot got upstairs to the visiting area, his lawyer was already there waiting for him inside the secure private visiting room, sitting down in a dark pen stripe suit with his legs crossed. The deputy shackled one of Jackpot's hands to a cuff that was attached to the table for the lawyers protection. *You can imagine how many people in the past, before they started cuffing you to the table, probably took off on their attorney and busted a nutty on the fool after he told them they was getting life in prison or some shit like that. Especially after paying an arm and a leg for their services,* Jackpot couldn't help but think to himself as they cuffed him to the table. Jackpot sat down and shook his lawyers hand as the deputy left the 2 to talk.

"Okay, as you know, Lisa's testimony hurt us. If she comes into trial with that same song-n-dance it's a high chance you'll lose this trial. The pictures that they confiscated from your home with you, her, and some of the other girls, help prove some of her statements. I saw the pictures and they're not good. Now with that being said, this D.A. is a bitch with a real hard on to take you down. It took a lot, but I was able to work out a sweet deal. The only reason she agreed was because she didn't want to put the girls back on the stand and cause them anymore heart ache and pain having to re-live their ordeal being with you."

Heart ache and pain my ass. Them bitches is full of more shit then a seagull. I bet they ass on the blade right now as we speak, with some tricks dick in their mouth faking the funk like life's sweet. Fuck them hoes! Jackpot thought to himself, but kept his mouth closed and finished listening to the offer his lawyer was trying to present.

"The D.A. agreed to 6 years with 1/2 and she'll run all the charges concurrent. With the time you already have in, and good time credits you'll earn in the penitentiary, that should put you out in 2005. Reject this offer, and we go to trial, flip the coin and take our chances."

As much as Jackpot didn't wanna go to the penitentiary, he was realistic and knew that it was no way he was gonna beat trial with Lisa on the stand. He also knew that the deal wasn't gonna get any better than this. "Fuckin bitch, I hope that hoe dies a thousand deaths," Jackpot said under his breath but could tell the lawyer heard him by the expression on his face. "Alright, tell the bitch I'll take the deal. Where do I sign?"

"I'll draw up the paperwork. You'll sign at your next court date in a week. From there things will move fast and you should be in the penitentiary by next month to start your sentence. Keep your head up, this is a sweet deal. It truly could be a lot worst." Jackpot wasn't feeling that bullshit his lawyer was saying and responded as such.

"Yeah that's easy for you to say. While you're at home for the next 3 holidays with your family, I'll be behind bars in a 5x9 box with 2 hots and a cot. Out of sight and out of mind." The lawyer responded to that with just a stupid look on his face. He knew Jackpot was right. He could never imagine himself in jail or prison. Not even for a day. He would hang himself first. Jackpot and his lawyer concluded their meeting. The deputy came in and escorted Jackpot back to his module.

Jackpot went back to his cell, laid on his bed, and thought about the shine before the storm. How did he go from being the biggest pimp in the world to inmate #7255500? Jackpot got up and called his mom and Yuki to tell them the news. His mom took it hard and Yuki took it harder. His mother was a spiritual person and always felt like god would see him through. There was no way her baby was going to prison. She kept the faith and truly felt that way.

But faith nor Jesus would keep Jackpot from going to the penitentiary. Satan won this battle, and it came in the form of a white girl from Ohio name Lisa. When Yuki heard the news she passed out. All Jackpot heard was the phone drop and a crash. Yuki landing on the living room coffee table as she fell, she hit the back of her head which put her in a coma. When she came through 8 weeks later, the doctor said she'd never be the same.

The hit to her head caused internal bleeding and slight brain damage. Yuki would spend the rest of her life with no control of the left side of her body in a wheel chair. 6 months after the news, Yuki killed herself with an overdose of sleeping pills. When Jackpot found out, he took the news hard and couldn't help but blame himself. For the first time in his life, he began to wish that he never chose the lifestyle he had. The big misconception is that a pimp has no feelings. But if a pimp had no feelings then he wouldn't be human. God gave us all feelings, but a pimp just knows how to conceal his. A good pimp doesn't work from the heart, but from the mind. The mind controls the body. There's a saying that goes...there's only 2 ways out of the pimp game. The penitentiary or the nut house, and Jackpot was beginning to feel like he might see both.

19 GAME OVER

It was a full month after hearing the tragic news about Yuki before Jackpot came out his cell. He still wasn't over her death, but he knew that he couldn't stay in his cell forever. He hadn't programed within the system in a month. Not even to go to chow. He would just lay on his bunk thinking about the first time he saw Yuki in a mall with her friends. How life would have been so different for her if they had never met.

"Was this my punishment for the lifestyle I chose to live all along knowing it was a sin?" Jackpot asked himself this question all the time. He thought about Green Eyes and how she got strung out on crystal after he got arrested. Although she was already hoe'n when they met, he still couldn't help but feel guilty or some what at fault for how she turned out. He thought about the first time Yuki stepped foot on the blade. The smile and look on her face when she broke luck the first time and handed him the money. He thought about how she stayed down to the bitter end and never turned her back on him. A slight smile would come across Jackpot's face when he pictured, and reminisced about some of the good times they shared. The holidays, exotic trips to the Bahamas and Jamaica. The look on her face when he bought her BMW and told her it was hers.

Jackpot use to love and pride himself in his mouthpiece. Now he resented and wish he never had it. Jackpot went to the yard and bought 2 sticks of weed, went back to his cell, put his Boys 2 Men CD in his radio, and bumped the track..."It's so hard to say goodbye to yesterday," from Coolie High. Jackpot lit a inscent wick to hide the smell of the stick (weed) he lit next, sat back on his bunk, and zoned out.

Jackpot was housed at Folsom State Penitentiary. New bodies was coming in when he looked down the tier and saw a familiar face. **"Jackson...cell 20-up,"** the C.O. said, as the convict with the familiar face stopped in front of Jackpot's cell. Jackpot still didn't recognize him but knew that he saw him somewhere before. *Maybe it was in the county or court where I saw him before,* Jackpot thought to himself. The cell door opened and the convict walked in with his bed roll.

"Wuss up wit it brother?... JP." Jackpot introduced himself. The convict answered back with a flashy grill that would've put Baby from Cash Money Records to shame. That's when it all clicked in. Jackpot knew exactly who this was. "Hold up. Not Fuk-A-Bitch?" That threw Jamal off at first because he didn't recognize Jackpot in his prison blues.

"Wut up pimp? It's Jackpot." JP said, realizing by the expression on F.A.B's face that at first he didn't recognize him or knew who he was. "Oh shit, get tha fuck outta here! Wuss up playa" They shook hands and gave each other a one arm bear hug. The 2 chopped it up for the next few hours, while puffing on the other stick that Jackpot had bought on the yard earlier that day.

Throughout their entire conversation, F.A.B's charges never came into play. At least not the details. He just said that he was down for a long while until his appeal went through. Jackpot learned a long time ago not to ask people about their case or how much time they had, so he never even pressed the issue. If F.A.B wanted to tell him what he was locked for, then he would tell him. If not, then that was his business, right, and prerogative.

"Man I'm just glad they put me in a cell wit a pimp like myself, instead of one of them gang bangin or square mutha fucka's."

"Yeah I feel you there. I ain't never been with the gang shit. Only thang I bang on is a bitch," Jackpot responded. Having F.A.B in his cell was like having a pimp doctor in there, sent to wash all his square thoughts and bullshit away. Chopping it up with F.AB was therapeutic. For a split second he actually forgot about Yuki.

For the rest of the night, they chopped it up about the game. Everything from, who was still out there doing it big, to who had lost all their hoes and fell off. Jackpot reminded him about the day they was at the stoplight, and when F.A.B broke Green Eyes for all her dough in Oakland. They both laughed about it as they remembered the day. They ended up talking all through the night, until chow call snapped them out of it. "Damn playa, we talked all night. What's it like, six o'clock?" F.A.B asked.

"Yep, pretty much. Chow time is at 6:30. They wake us up at 6 to get ready." Jackpot said as they got up and got ready to head to the chow hall.

------$$$$------

It had been 6 months since F.A.B arrived at Folsom. In the time that he'd been there, him and Jackpot had gotten real close. So close, that one afternoon after yard sitting in the dayroom, he decided to tell Jackpot what he was locked up for. "Yeah pimp, you know it's really fuck a bitch wit me all the way. They don't call me that shit fa'nuttin. I'll leave a bitch in a ditch quick wit the maggots and ticks." F.A.B spoke as the two talked about the game like most seasoned pimps do to keep their game sharp.

"Yeah, I use ta hear about how you use to put the gorilla fist down from town to town."

"You damn right pimp. A hoe ain't shit, and I pimp by the book. They should've called me Fuk-A-Bitch Slim, cause Iceberg would have been proud. You see, look here pimp. I ain't the one to be laid up wit a whore and catering to her needs. That's what them tricks is for. A hoe I know is either gonna pay me, or pay me no attention. I'm cut from a 70's cloth. These pimps now a days be laid up wit the hoe and catching feelings. What part of the game is that? Maybe it's checkers you know, got the king running squares cause it definitely ain't pimpin." F.A.B was on one. He was in his pimp zone, so Jackpot listened to him talk. "A hoe is dumber than a pimp, but smarter than a square and sharper than a trick. So when the bitch catches the 1st sign of weakness in her pimp, she gets laxed. She tries to exploit the fact and use it to her advantage. The bitch starts getting lazy and coming in wit funny money. She starts running hoes up out the stable then play the roll like she don't know why they left. Now she looking good in her pimps eyes because she still around and holding it down. A sucka pimp a forget it's cop-n-blow, touch-n-go, fall for the bullshit, and put the hoe up on a pedestal.

"Now the bitch know she got her folks where she wants him, dependent on her funky ass. She starts tryna con and run game day ta day on her folks like she does her tricks. She gets bold. Now she's hiding money and bringing home ones and nones, two's and fews. The pimp can't understand how, his once top money maker is now his worst. He believes her when she says it's slow. She knows he will because she used the drag before, and the sucka believed her without putting a foot in her ass. Now every other day it's so called slow.

"The bitch is working his mind like a trick and he don't even know it. He can't keep his dick out of her. He keeps the hoe pussy sorer than work does. She's basically getting rewarded for nothing, so where's the motivation to work? There is none. The pimp never ruled wit an iron fist, so she tries him. She calls his bluff. She doesn't believe him when he says he's gonna kick her ass. It's like a parent that always say they're gonna beat their bad ass child for fuckin up. At first they take you serious and it scares the shit out of them, so momentarily they straighten up. But one too many waves of the belt and no ass whooping, they began to realize you ain't finna do shit. You're just bluffing, like a chihuahua nipping at your ankles and showing his teeth. He's pimpin wit feelings, and that shit never works. In the pimp game, it's better to be feared then loved. I don't give a fuck if a bitch love me or not. Just love this pimpin. And when a bitch break my rules, I'm a break her fuckin neck."

Jackpot knew that F.A.B made a lot of sense. Even though he didn't agree with all his tactics, he knew that most of them was necessary. Shit, if Lisa had feared him he probably wouldn't be sitting in prison right now. The way you start a relationship is the way you end a relationship. He started on some sweet shit, so it ended on some sweet shit. Yeah he was a die hard pimp, but he did it all from the lip. And even a hoe is smart enough to realize after a while that it's all talk.

"Yeah I can dig it to a certain extent," Jackpot said, then finished. "Because even the best mouth piece is bound to repeat itself. Not only that, but your hoes that been around for a while hear you getting at some of the new and other bitches with some of that same spit and began to realize it's all game. The pimpin stops being a mystery to them. They start putting pieces together and figured out the game like a jigsaw puzzle. Now they began to feel bamboozled, played. They began to realize that there's no big ass pot of gold at the end of the rainbow, and never was.

"They start soaking up the same game the pimps been spitting to them. They think they got the pimp figured out. Now they feel like they can reverse the game back on him. This is why a pimp should know how to re-invent himself. He should always have something new to say. It's about conversation and persuasion. But when you're out here connect the dot pimpin from a book and these movies with the same old tired lines a hoe done heard a thousand times, it's not gonna work. Or your pimpin's gonna be stagnated. Be a macker not a rapper. Just because you can put a few lines together in a clever way don't make you a pimp. Most nigga's today is pimpin backwards if you ask me. Put down the Iceberg Slim and Donald Goins books. That shit was written in the 60's and was based on the 40's and 50's. Nigga, this is mutha fuckin 2000!

"Put a hanger and boot to a bitch if you wanna, and find yourself rotten away in one of these cold gray cells. Quit watching pimp videos of clowns talking it but ain't walking it. Nigga's pushing dope an pussy then saying it all came out of a bitches cock when it's not. Fool, quit pimpatrating and straddling the fence. A real pimp only sale pussy, no cut. **Period!** Put down your gun and pick up your pimp stick and quit banging on the track. That shit ain't pimpin. The Bloods and Crips got that market sold up. Let em have it. Quit cross hustling. If I said it once I'll say it twice, a pimp just pimp! Nigga, quit popping X-pills with your hoe and freaking all weekend, she looking at you like a trick."

"Preach!" F.A.B responded as Jackpot continued.

"Ain't no wonder these hoes now a days be outta pocket and disrespecting pimpin. Tryna work on their own and acting grown. Coming to court snitching and pointing at pimpin. The game is changing pimp, and I can't necessarily say for the better either. I love this game like I love my mother, but pimpin ain't been pimpin right, and hoes haven't been wrapped too tight for a while now."

"Tell me about it. Why you think I said you have to keep a foot in their ass at all times? What you think I'm here for?" F.A.B said then answered his own question. "For killing a hoe that tried to leave."

"What!" Jackpot said, in disbelief. He couldn't see himself spending the rest of his life in prison behind a bitch that wanted to leave him. That wasn't pimpin, that was murder. Then it dawned on him like the morning sky. Jamal Jackson was the person he read about in county jail that killed his hoe in Oakland. He always knew that the name "Jamal Jackson" sounded familiar but never put 2 and 2 together and figured it out. "Yep, remember that Sunshine bitch I knocked from you?"

"Yeah, what about her?" Jackpot responded, still not fully catching on to what F.A.B was saying. "You won't have to be bitter or upset about her leaving you because I can 100% tell you without a doubt, you was the last nigga she left breathing." Jackpot couldn't believe what he was hearing. Even though Sunshine left Jackpot high and dry and went to another pimp, he wouldn't wish death upon her. Shit, that was part of the game. You win some, you lose some.

If you're slackin in your mackin then your hoe's heels is gonna get ta clackin. *Clowns like this is what gives the game a black eye quicker than a Tyson fight,* Jackpot thought to himself, looking at the sinister and unremorseful smile on F.A.B's face as Jackpot's body began to fill with rage. "All in the name of pimpin huh?" Jackpot asked, with a disgusted look on his face. He never pimped with his heart, but he cared for Sunshine. "You god damn right pimp. No hoe just gon walk away from me after I laced her with this mackin. If she does, it's gonna be in a body bag. She wasn't the 1st, but she damn sure was the last. I done bodied 10 hoes in my lifetime before her." F.A.B's hate for hoes came from when he was young. A little kid, not even 10 years old.

His mother was a whore and very abusive towards him when she drank and got high. F.A.B was a Trick Baby. He never knew his father. His mother didn't know who his father was either, but she had enough sense to know who's it wasn't. It wasn't the love child of a caring loving man or husband, because that man didn't exist. The only men his mother been with when he was conceived was rich white tricks. F.A.B's good hair and light eyes was a constant reminder of the fact.

When she looked in her sons face, she would resent and despise him. Every time she got drunk, and even worst when she got high. Once he turned 6, the beatings came. She would call him a Trick Baby and a fuck wasted. She would tell him that he was the reason for her struggles. That she wished that she had given him up when he was young.

This was F.A.B's childhood up until his 10th birthday when his mother overdosed on heroin. F.A.B awoke to his mother laying on the couch slouched over with a needle still in her arm, eyes rolled in the back of her head, foaming at the mouth. This is the reason why to this day, F.A.B doesn't celebrate his birthday. After his mothers death, F.A.B was taken to a foster home where he grew up and stayed at until he was 18.

F.A.B's childhood memories made him hate his mother, and hate hoes even more. When he saw a hoe, he saw his mother. When he beat the shit out of a bitch, he was getting his mother back for all the beatings she had laid upon him. F.A.B's mind was warped, but it made for a good pimp. A deadly ice cold, no nonsense, die hard pimp. One that didn't even love his own momma, so how the fuck was he gonna love a bitch? F.A.B started pimpin when he was 19 and killed his first hoe when he was 20. This nigga put the gorilla in pimpin. "I ain't wit that shit. That ain't pimpin to me. I'm all for being hard on a bitch, but I ain't finna kill a hoe over no punk shit like that," Jackpot said, faced frowned up, not feeling the bullshit F.A.B was saying. "So wut choo saying nigga, you got heart for a hoe?"

"I'm saying, the game's about choice, not force. Ain't nothing pimpin bout dat nigga."

"Nigga, if you got feelings you should have been a bitch and quit claiming to be a pimp." Jackpot took off on F.A.B an punched him in the face. Calling a man a bitch in prison was like signing a death sentence. You could get away with calling a man a piece of shit before you got away with calling him a bitch. F.A.B regrouped, got his composure, then punched him back. The watchful eye in the gun tower couldn't see what was taking place due to them being in a blind spot. If he had, you could rest assure he would have shot first and asked questions last.

F.A.B being the grimy nigga he is, pulled out a shank and rushed Jackpot. Jackpot had no choice but to pull his. Now they was in a knife fight. Jackpot stepped to the side as F.A.B came rushing in and stuck em in the neck. **The death blow!** F.A.B dropped to his knees, dropped the shank, and fell on his stomach. Jackpot quickly wiped his shank off with a homemade doo–rag and dropped it near the body. Jackpot quickly put some distance between him and Fuk–A–Bitch and went towards his cell. 2 seconds later he would have been caught. No sooner than he got away from the body, the alarm went off. **"Yard down, yard down...Everybody get the fuck down!!!"** The C.O. in the gun tower holding the M–14 said, after noticing what appeared to be a dead inmate on the ground leaking blood. A dozen or so C.O.'s rushed the building. They searched and questioned everybody present before sending them back to their cells and locking them down. In prison, you live by 3 rules. See no evil, hear no evil, speak no evil. So no one saw shit, heard shit, and most importantly...said shit! Jackpot got away with murder.

He was happy he didn't turn his 6 years with 1/2 into a life sentence. For the next 2 years, Jackpot stayed to himself and out of the mix. He saw countless youngsters come though talking about they pimpin. He paid then no mind and never hipped them to who he was. These young nigga's was on some new sneaker tennis shoe pimp shit. The new breed traded in their now-or-later gators for multi colored Air Force 1's and Babe and Apes.

Jackpot just finished up his time playing chess and reading books. At times, he would think about Yuki and Sunshine. When Yuki passed, Jackpot used the money for his bail bondsman to pay for her funeral and tombstone. He had his mother take care of the arrangements. Knowing that he was Yuki's only family in the U.S. He felt it was the right thing to do.

November 2005

Jackpot paroled from prison. He had $200 and the clothes on his back. He had lost everything to the game. He was hoeless, homeless, and broke. Jackpot's mother had died during his last 6 months in prison. He took the news hard. For some reason,

CDC (California Department of Corrections) wouldn't allow Jackpot to attend her funeral. Something about his custody points being too high. His mother had died from a sudden rare form of cancer. She didn't even know that she was sick. At the time she was diagnosed, she looked and appeared healthy.

Prison officials dropped JP off at the Greyhound bus depot where he bought a one way ticket back to San Diego. On the ride home, Jackpot thought about his life, and his life within the game with deep regret. He was now everything he always said he'd never be. An ex-pimp with a bunch of stories, a lot of game, and nothing to show for it. This was the reality of the game. Rarely is there ever a happy ending. Very few live to tell their tales or retire a rich man with happy hoes. Rosebud showed you the reality of a pimps future in the movie documentary "American Pimp."

For every pimp that die or fall off, there's another to take his place. The game's been around since the beginning of time, and will continue straight ahead into the next ice age. Jackpot arrived in Daygo at 3 p.m. The first thing he did was visit Yuki and his moms grave. The 2 women that meant the most to him in his life laid side by side. On Yuki's tombstone it read...**May you always be remembered and never forgotten, Till Game Do Us Part.**

The End

A HUSTLERS POEM

My mind stays strong as I sit in a cell
Reminiscing about home but now my home is jail
In a five by nine box, feel like the walls are closing
Out of sight, out of mine, now no one knows him
Family, friends, and loves ones, they all fell off
I say a prayer to calm my thoughts as I'm gripping
the cross
Till game do us part was the phrase of the day
Until they locked up the hustler and took him away
Now the ones he loved the most, they all went
astray
The more he thinks about his life, he can see it was
all fake
The money, power, and respect, it came with a
price
Even his own so called girlfriends won't pick up a
pen and write
Excuses is useless and everyones got em
Now life for everyone he knew, is so complicated
without him
What's Bonnie without Clyde, a Pimp without his
Bottom?
Making love pillow talking she said she couldn't live
without him
The cars, clothes and homes, she would have never
had without him

When he was on the streets she trust an believe in
him, but now that he's locked up, she's constantly
doubting him
What goes around comes back around and karma's
a bitch
It's women in his life like this that got him saying
"Trust No Bitch"
No matter how good of a person you are, a snitch is
a snitch
which is why now a days you can't even trust half of
the people you come in contact with
In a five by nine box, feel like the walls are closing
out of sight, out of mind, now no one knows him
Visits few and far, the man repo'd your car
Now it's inmate #T-23693 doing time where life is
hard
Before you got locked, everyone said how they
loved you so much
Now them same ones that love you can't even keep
in touch
Take a hustler down and another pops up to fill his
shoes
From tailor made suits to sitting in county blues
My mind stays strong as I sit in a cell
Reminiscing about home but now my home is jail
Out of sight, out of mind, smile now cry later
The world's a lonely place, for the life of a Player

Caujuan Akim Mayo

ABOUT THE AUTHOR

Caujuan Akim Mayo, also known on the streets as $ki.Bo and Ka$hanova, grew up hustling at a young age to make ends meet and help his single mother take care of his sister and 5 brothers. Early on, he had a way with words and women and found himself engulfed within the "Game" and lifestyle of The Pimping and Hoe subculture. The same game that brought him up, eventually took him down and sent him to prison.

There, is where he found a knack and love for writing and penned his first novel, "Let Me Pimp Or Let Me Die." With part 2 already finished, and another book on the way, Caujuan turned his negative situation into a positive one. After being released from prison, He turned his life around, started Uprock Publications, self published his novel, gave up the pimp game, and started giving back to the community in a positive way.

• Website: www.letmepimporletmedie.com
• Emails: caujuan@gmail.com
• Facebook: caujuan
• Twitter: caujuan

<u>COMING SOON</u>

LET ME PIMP OR LET ME DIE 2
=The hoe chronicles=

MY SKIN IS MY SIN THE DIARY OF A GANGSTA
=Inspired by a true story=